The Land of
Far-Beyond

The Land of
Far-Beyond

Enid Blyton

Illustrated by Horace Knowles

Dragon

Granada Publishing Limited
Published in 1970 by Dragon Books
Frogmore, St Albans, Herts AL2 2NF
Reprinted 1971, 1974

First published by Methuen & Co Ltd 1942
Copyright Enid Blyton 1942
Made and printed in Great Britain by
C. Nicholls & Company Ltd
The Philips Park Press, Manchester
Set in Monotype Times

INTRODUCTION

Many years ago a man called John Bunyan wrote the adventures of Christian, a pilgrim, in a book called *The Pilgrim's Progress*. Some of you may have read this book, or tried to read it. It is in difficult language, and many of the ideas are hard for children of nowadays to follow.

Now, in this book, I have written for you a kind of new *Pilgrim's Progress*, in my own words, and with my own quite different ideas. It cannot really be compared with the old *Pilgrim's Progress*, but I thought you might like to know that it was this grand old book that gave me the idea of writing a completely new one for you. I hope you will enjoy following the many strange adventures of the children from the City of Turmoil to the Land of Far-Beyond.

You will be able to act a great deal of this story if you want to.

ENID BLYTON

HORACE KNOWLES

CHAPTER ONE

THE CITY OF TURMOIL

Once upon a time, in the great City of Turmoil, there lived three children. One was a boy called Peter, and his sisters were Anna and Patience.

The City of Turmoil was a great, noisy, dirty place, full of streets, houses, shops, and market-places. The children wandered about, looking at everything, playing games in the streets and the parks, and only going home when it was dark, or when they were hungry.

There were schools, of course, but the children went to school only when they thought of it. Their mother and father let them do exactly as they liked, just as most of the other children in the city did.

"Let's go to school to-day, for a change!" said Peter to his sisters one day. "It's story-time to-day. It *is* Wednesday, isn't it?"

"Oh, don't let's go to *school*!" cried Anna. "I've thought of a lovely thing we can do. Let's go down Twisty Street, and ring the bells there, and run away. Then people will come to the door – and nobody will be there!"

"Oh, yes!" said Patience, dancing round. "That would be fun. Come on! I don't want to go to school."

"You look very dirty," said their mother. "Have you washed this morning? And Patience, you really must mend that hole in your dress."

The children took no notice. Children hardly ever did take any notice of their parents in the City of Turmoil. They just grew up as they pleased and did what they liked.

They ran off. They came to Twisty Street and called to the other children they met.

"John! Lily! We're going to ring bells. Come and see us!"

Two or three more children came along, giggling. "This is where Miss Crosspatch lives," said Peter, running up the steps of a tall house. "Now, hide, you others!"

The children scattered behind a cart as Peter tugged at the bell. A peal sounded through the tall house. Peter fled down the steps and joined the other children.

7

The door opened and a thin, tall woman with spectacles on her nose looked out. She was astonished to see no one there.

"I feel sure I heard the bell," she said to herself, and shut the door again. The children giggled, and Peter sped up the steps of the tall house again. He tugged hard at the bell – jangle-jangle, it could even be heard by the children hidden behind the cart.

Peter ran down the steps at top speed and crouched behind the cart, laughing. The door opened, and an angry face looked out. Still nobody there!

"It's those children again!" said Miss Crosspatch, frowning. "Wait till I catch them; I'll box their horrid little ears!"

She slammed the door. The milkman came up the street, whistling. He had some butter and eggs for Miss Crosspatch, and he rang the bell.

"Jangle-jangle!" Nobody came to open the door. The children hugged themselves for joy. Miss Crosspatch thought it was some naughty boy again, of course! The milkman rang again, and again – and then again. The door opened suddenly, and Miss Crosspatch appeared, quite certain that the bell was being rung by children. She smacked the milkman hard on the cheek, and he dropped the eggs and butter in amazement.

"Now look here!" he said, in a rage. "Now look here!"

"Oh!" said Miss Crosspatch, looking at the bag of broken eggs, and the packet of butter on the steps. "Oh – I thought you were some naughty children! Look, there they are, the tiresome wretches!"

The cart had suddenly moved away and Miss Crosspatch had caught sight of the five children who had been hiding behind it. She ran down the steps towards them. But they could run much faster than she could, and were away at the end of the street long before she had got half-way down.

"That was fun," said Patience, stopping to do up her broken shoe-lace. "Really, that was fun!"

"Let's ring one more bell!" said Anna. "I'll do it this time!" So up the steps of another house she ran and pulled at the bell. She ran down the steps again and hid with the others behind a fence.

A maid came to the door, and looked angrily up and down the road. "The children are getting worse and worse!" they heard her say as she banged the door.

"What shall we do now?" said Peter. "I feel rather hungry."

There was a shout from the next street, and the children turned to see some more boys and girls that they knew.

"Hie! Come along with us! There's a barrow of fruit down here!"

"Good!" said the five, and tore off to join two bigger boys. They were bad boys, who stole from shops and barrows.

"You come and help us," said Ron and William, the boys. "See that man with the barrow there? Well, we want two of you to help us, and we'll be able to get as much fruit as we want to."

"That's stealing, and the policeman might get us," said Patience.

"Pooh! Don't be a coward!" said Ron. "Now listen – which of you are the fastest runners?"

"Peter and Anna," said Patience. "They run like the wind."

"Well, Peter and Anna, you must run up to the barrow and dance round it, calling out rude named to the man," said Ron. "You must make him so angry that he'll chase you. As soon as he's gone we'll run up and help ourselves to the fruit – and we'll share it with you when you come back."

"All right," said Peter. "But I hope we don't get caught! Come on!"

Peter and Anna ran up to the barrow. The other children hid behind the corner, watching, waiting for their chance. Peter began to dance round the barrow, keeping out of reach of the man in charge of it.

"Hallo, pie-face! Hallo, stick-in-the-mud! Hallo, slowcoach! Can't catch me, can't catch me!"

"Go away, rude boy," said the man, and tried to slap Peter. But Peter dodged out of the way. Then it was Anna's turn.

"Your apples are bad! Your pears are all maggotty! Your flowers are falling to bits – and so are you!" sang the rude little girl. The man ran round the barrow after her.

"I won't have you children cheeking me like this!" he shouted. Peter put out a foot and the man tripped over and fell to the ground with a crash. His face was red with rage when he got up. "I'll whip you both for this!" he cried.

"Can't catch me, can't catch me!" shouted Peter, rudely putting his tongue out. The man ran after him. Peter sped off down the street, in the opposite direction to that in which the other children had planned to run. Anna ran too, and the man, muttering to himself, tore after them, quite determined to catch them and punish them.

As soon as he was safely down the street the other children ran out from their hiding-place. But when they got to the barrow only Ron and William dared to take the fruit. The two boys crammed their pockets full, keeping an eye on the running man.

He had nearly caught Peter and Anna. They shouted to him, "Look what's happening to your fruit!"

He turned – and when he saw the children round his barrow, with Ron and William helping themselves, he gave an angry shout and ran back up the street, leaving Anna and Peter to dance about in glee.

When Ron and William saw him coming they raced off with the others, and were soon safely round the corner. The poor man didn't know what to do! If he chased them, he was afraid that Peter and Anna would run up and help themselves – so there was nothing for him to do but to stand by his barrow and say the rudest things he could think of about the children of the City of Turmoil!

Peter and Anna ran round another way and joined the other five children. They found a great quarrel going on. Ron and William would not share with any of the others!

"No!" said Ron. "*We* got the stuff. None of you others helped yourselves, you were such sillies. Well, you can't expect us to give you any, then."

"You *are* mean!" said Patience, fiercely. "You promised to share!"

"Well, why should we keep a promise?" asked William. "It's only stupids who keep promises! Nobody keeps promises any more. You shouldn't have believed us. We're not giving you any of this fruit at all."

Then there began such a fight! Patience slapped Ron on the cheek, and Lily scratched William on the hand. John and Peter gave both boys a hard punch, but the bigger boys soon sent all the children flying. Then off they went with their pockets crammed full of fruit, to eat it in a safe corner.

"The beasts!" said Anna, beginning to cry. "I shall have a bruise where Ron hit me."

"Oh, don't be a cry-baby," said John. "What shall we do now? Look – there's a dog nosing round that dustbin. Let's throw something at it!"

The children picked up anything they could find and threw it at the thin, half-starved little dog. A stone hit him on the head, and he yelped in pain. Another hit him on the back and he turned to run. But the bad children had surrounded him, and he could not see any way of escape.

A big clod of earth struck one of his back legs. He began to

"POOR FELLOW," SAID THE STRANGER, IN A DEEP, KIND VOICE.
"POOR FELLOW! WHAT HAS HAPPENED TO YOU?"

limp. He snapped at Peter and got away between the boy's legs. He limped off down the road, yelping in pain.

And then the Stranger appeared. He came walking round the corner, and saw the limping dog at once. He called to it, and it ran to him on its three legs.

"Who's that?" whispered Patience to Anna. "I've never seen him before. Isn't he queer?"

The Stranger was only queer because he was so clean and neat and lovely to look at. He wore a short tunic of white, and his feet were shod with sandals. His legs were wound about with thongs of leather. He bent over the dog and lifted up the hurt leg. It was bleeding.

"Poor fellow," said the Stranger, in a deep, kind voice. "Poor fellow! What has happened to you?"

The dog wagged its stump of a tail, and licked the Stranger's hand. The man looked up at the children. "I must bathe this dog's leg," he said. "Where is there some water?"

"There's a river down the end of that road," said Peter. The boy wanted to run away before the man found out that it was he who had wounded the dog on the leg, but the Stranger seemed so extraordinary and mysterious that he felt he had to stay and watch him.

"Hasn't he got a shining face?" said Anna.

"And what deep, gleaming eyes!" said Lily. "I like him. I wouldn't run away from him as I would from most grown-ups here. And fancy him bothering about a dog! I've never seen any one fussing a dog before!"

"Come and show me the river," said the tall Stranger, looking at the children with his deep eyes, that shone like a blue pool. And obediently the five children guided him down the street to where the big river flowed along.

CHAPTER TWO

THE STRANGER. THE TERRIBLE BURDENS.
THE BEGINNING OF A LONG JOURNEY

The children went down the steps to the beach, for the river was low at that time. The Stranger carried the dog in his arms, and they watched him whilst he bathed its leg. He said comforting things to it, and the children were astonished. They had never been taught to be kind to animals, and when they saw a cat, dog, or bird, their first thought was always to throw something at it!

"I wonder who hurt you," said the Stranger, as he bound up the leg with a strip of linen torn from his handkerchief. "This is a dreadful City! I have seen horses slashed for not going up hills quickly enough. I have seen cats so thin that they can surely only live on what is in dustbins, and cannot have good homes. I have seen dirty, ragged children who should be at school – children with no manners, no kindness in them, whose hard little faces have no beauty. I have seen grown-ups careless and dishonest, selfish and hard – how can the children learn to be anything else! How I wish I had never left my own land!"

The children listened as the Stranger talked to himself and the dog. "Where do you come from?" asked Anna, boldly.

"I come from the Land of Far-Beyond," said the Stranger. "My name is Wanderer, but my home is there. I cannot stay in one place for long. I have to see what the world is like, and take the news back to my own land. I heard many things of the great City of Turmoil, so I came to see it on my way to the country beyond. But I wish I had never come here. It is a city of great burdens!"

"Great burdens! What do you mean?" asked Peter, scornfully. "A burden is a load, isn't it? There are no burdens in our city."

"You all carry a terrible burden in your hearts," said the Stranger, sadly. "The burden of selfishness, untruthfulness, dishonesty, uncleanliness, deceit, greed, disloyalty – ah, I could tell you many, many more. Your hearts must be heavy, even as mine is light. Have I seen a happy or a kind face since I first entered this city? Not one!"

"*I* haven't got a burden," said Peter. "You are talking nonsense, Stranger!"

The Stranger looked at him out of his deep eyes, and Peter felt uncomfortable. "You are only a boy," said the tall man. "But you have a terrible burden already! Ah, if you could see that burden, how astonished and dismayed you would be!"

"You are telling fibs!" said Peter, rudely. "You show me my burden if you can! I'll believe you then!"

"Show me mine, too!" cried Anna.

"And mine!" said Patience. The other children said nothing. The felt a little frightened, for the Stranger's eyes gleamed with such a curious light.

I can show you your burdens if you like," said the Stranger, slowly. "But if I do, you will feel their dreadful weight."

"Go on. Show us!" cried Anna, impatiently.

"Shut your eyes, and think of nothing!" said Wanderer, commandingly, looking at the three children in turn. "Empty your minds so that I may fill them with good and beautiful thoughts, that will push from your heart the evil burden there!"

The children did as they were told. They stood there, with their eyes shut, thinking of nothing. And into their heads came thoughts they had never known – thoughts of loving-kindness, thoughts of beauty, shining, wonderful thoughts – and at the same time a pain came round their hearts, as the burden they carried there of wrong and shameful things began to move and writhe.

"Open your eyes!" commanded the Stranger in such a sad voice that the children opened their eyes in amazement. Why was he so unhappy?

They felt a terrible weight on their backs, a weight that almost dragged them down. Anna groaned.

"Oh, what's the matter with me!" she cried, trying to see what was on her back.

"It is your burden," said Wanderer. "The burden that you did not believe in. The burden of all the ugly things you have said and done and thought in your life!"

"Oh, Peter has a burden, too; a great load on his back!" cried Lily, staring in wonder at a great burden across Peter's shoulders. "Peter, isn't it terribly heavy?"

"Yes," said Peter, trying to straighten his shoulders. "Wanderer, I believe you now. Take this load away from me. I can't bear it."

"I cannot take it away," said Wanderer. "It can only be taken from you if you go to the Land of Far-Beyond, and reach my city, the City of Happiness. No one can take it away from you here."

Peter, Patience, and Anna stared at the Stranger in horror and dismay.

"We haven't got to carry these loads all the time, have we?" cried Anna. "Oh, do, do take them away. You made them come. You can surely take them away."

"I didn't make them come," said Wanderer. "*You* made them yourselves. I only gave them shape, to show you how heavy they were."

The children began to cry bitterly, for they were frightened.

14

Some grown-ups, attracted by the little crowd, came down the steps to see what was the matter. Peter saw that one was a friend of his mother's.

"Miss Grumble! Tell this man to take away this load from my back!" he begged her. "He made it come! Tell him to take it away!"

Lily explained what had happened and the grown-ups listened in amazement. They tried to take the burdens from the backs of the three children but they cried out in pain. "Don't! Don't! It hurts when you try to pull them away."

"The burdens are their own, as much a part of them as their hair and their nails," said Wanderer, gravely. "You cannot remove them. They can only lose them by going to the Land of Far-Beyond, through difficult ways and hard paths. Otherwise they must carry them for the rest of their lives – and, alas, they will grow bigger and bigger, for there is no chance of losing a burden of this kind, in the wicked City of Turmoil."

The grown-ups laughed. One of them, Mr. Scornful, challenged Wanderer to produce a burden on his back too. "I suppose you think I've a burden of sin in *my* heart too!" he said. "Well, I haven't! I am a happy man, rich and powerful, with a big house and many horses. *I* have no burden! You cannot do your tricks on *me*!"

Wanderer looked round at the group of five grown-ups and five children. "You shall each see your burdens," he said, and every one fell silent. They shut their eyes when he commanded, their minds became empty, and a pain began to stir around their hearts, just as it had done before with the three children. And lo and behold when they opened their eyes again, each one of them was weighted down with a great burden on his back. And the biggest one of all was that on Mr. Scornful's shoulders!

"So you are a happy man?" said Wanderer, sadly, looking at the dismayed Mr. Scornful. "You did not feel the weight of the dishonest ways in which you got your money. You did not feel the burden of your scorn for other's feelings, your selfishness that made you trample others under so that *you* might get the wealth and power you wanted. Now you know the burden you carried in your hard heart!"

The dog came and licked Wanderer's hand. It still limped on three legs. "We must go," said Wanderer, patting the dog. "You will come with me, little friend? Good-bye, poor beasts of burden. Carry your loads as best you may, and do not add to them, or you will limp like this dog all your life long!"

He picked up his staff and went up the steps of the embankment. The group stared at him, and then Mr. Scornful called after him.

"Don't leave us like this! You must help us! We can't go about with these loads on our backs."

"Then go to the Land of Far-Beyond, and get rid of them!" called back the Stranger. "Leave the city by the west gate, and make for the hill you will see in the distance. Good-bye!"

Mr. Scornful started after him, clambering up the steps with difficulty. The others climbed up too. They tried to run after Wanderer, and they shouted loudly. He stood still and looked back at them, the dog by his side, wagging his tail.

"Take us with you!" cried Mr. Scornful, who somehow felt that this man with the shining face was the only person who could possibly help him. "Let us travel with you. Take us to the Land of Far-Beyond!"

"I cannot do that," said Wanderer. "You will travel so slowly with the burdens on your backs. I must go swiftly. Set out in a company, keep together, and help one another. Farewell for the last time!"

He disappeared down the street, taking long strides, the dog running beside him on three legs. Peter, Anna, and Mr. Scornful tried to run after him – but it was impossible to run far with their great burdens. They stopped, panting.

"Maybe our burdens will disappear in the night," said Mr. Scornful, who could hardly believe that such a queer thing could happen to him. "Let us all go home. If our loads are still with us in the morning, we will meet here and discuss what had better be done. This is a strange and terrible thing to happen."

The party split up and went slowly back to their different homes. Anna, Patience, and Peter went to tell their mother what had happened, but she could not believe what they said, and thought that they were making up a tale for her. She tried to wrench their burdens from their backs, and they shouted with pain.

"Mother, don't! It hurts. Our burdens are part of us. The Stranger said so. Let us lie down and sleep. We are so tired. To-morrow perhaps these burdens will have gone."

The three children lay down on their beds. They could not undress. They could not lie very comfortably because their burdens seemed to get in the way.

In the morning, alas, the loads were still there! The children wept as they ate their breakfast. What was to become of them?

THEY PASSED UNDER THE STONE ARCHWAY, AND FOUND
THEMSELVES OUTSIDE THE CITY

17

They must leave the City of Turmoil and try to find the Land of Far-Beyond. There was nothing else to do. They could neither work nor play with such burdens on their backs.

It was the same with the other seven. John and Lily still had their burdens, and the five grown-ups had theirs too. Mr. Scornful's had even grown a little bigger, because he had lost his temper half the night, and had added to his burden. With solemn, grave faces they met beside the river.

There were the five children – Peter, Anna, Patience, John, and Lily. There was Mr. Scornful. There was his brother, Mr. Fearful, and his cousin, Miss Simple. There was another man, a young one, called Dick Cowardly, and his sister, Gracie Grumble. The little group looked at one another and their burdens, and then the grown-ups talked together, deciding what they and the five children were to do.

"There is only one thing to do," said Mr. Scornful. "We must try to find our way to the Land of Far-Beyond. After all, if that stranger was able to come here from that land, then we can surely go there. We will all go together. I have plenty of money to buy food and shelter. We will start out this very morning."

"We have to go by the west gate," said Gracie Grumble. "Oh, dear, of course it would be the one farthest from here! Well, let's start."

They set off down the streets, a sorry company, going slowly because of the heavy weight on their backs. People stared at them as they went, and wondered where they were going. At last they reached the big west gate. They passed under the stone archway, and found themselves outside the city. The noise died away as they stood there, trying to see the hill to which they had to go.

"I've no doubt we shall find some one there who will give us more directions," said Mr. Scornful. "Look – there is the hill. It doesn't look very far. We must cheer up, for maybe the Land of Far-Beyond is not so far away as we think!"

They set off down a winding path that led in the direction of the distant hill. It reared its head against the sky, and seemed very high. Peter thought sadly that it would be very tiring to climb the hill with such a burden on his back.

"Come along," he said to Anna, holding out his hand. "We must keep together. Maybe we will have plenty of adventures on the way to the Land of Far-Beyond!"

CHAPTER THREE

THE RIVER TROUBLE. THE FORD OF DETERMINATION. MR. FEARFUL IS LEFT BEHIND

The little company tried to go as quickly as they could. The children, used to running and dancing around, found it very hard to carry such heavy weights on their backs. Gracie Grumble made a terrible fuss.

"Oh, that such a thing should happen to me!" she kept sighing. "That wicked man! How dare he try his tricks on me!"

"I do hope we shan't meet any great dangers," said her brother, Dick Cowardly. I'm sorry I had to leave my job in the city. It was well-paid, and now here I am, going off on dangerous adventures! I don't like it."

"Don't be such a ninny," said Mr. Scornful, in his sneering voice. "I've plenty of money to help us along. As long as you are with me you'll be all right."

"Are you quite sure about that?" asked his brother, Mr. Fearful, looking all round as if he expected a lion or tiger to leap out at him at any moment. "I feel like Dick – I don't like this sort of thing."

"Oh, come! Everything is sure to be all right, my dears!" said Miss Simple, in a bright voice. "Clouds have a silver lining, you know. We shall soon lose our burdens."

"I hope we shall," said Peter, feeling that his was getting very heavy indeed, as he walked along in the hot sun. "I've always wanted adventures – but not with a burden like this on my back!"

The little company travelled on, over a common upon which the summer sun blazed hotly. Gracie grumbled the whole time, and every one got very tired of her. At last they made her walk by herself, so that they could not hear her grumbling. When the sun was high, Mr. Scornful halted.

"It's about time we had a meal," he said. "Has any one brought anything to eat or drink? There don't seem to be any inns here that we could get food from."

None of the children had thought of bringing anything, though Peter had some chocolate he had forgotten about in his pocket. Gracie Grumble had brought a parcel of food, and so had Mr. Fearful, who was always afraid he might be hungry. So he had brought quite a large supply of sandwiches, and some bottles of lemonade.

"I've got something too," said Mr. Scornful, and he took a kit-bag from the top of his burden. "I didn't think many of you would remember we might want food and not be able to buy it for some while. So I've brought plenty."

The whole company sat down and the children were delighted to eat and drink. Gracie didn't like lemonade, and she turned up her nose at the ham sandwiches that Mr. Fearful offered her.

"Well, don't have them, then," said Mr. Fearful, handing them to the children instead. "And go and drink at that stream over there, if you don't want my lemonade."

They all rested a little after their meal, and then Mr. Scornful stood up. "We must start off again," he said. "We want to get to some kind of inn before nightfall. Come along, Gracie – and you children."

"Oh, can't we have a bit longer rest?" groaned Gracie, who was half-asleep.

"Well, you'll be left behind if you do," said Mr. Scornful. "What a misery you are, always groaning and grumbling about something!"

On went the ten people, the children going a little ahead, for their burdens were not so heavy as those of the grown-ups, and they could go faster. They chattered together as they went.

"I'm getting a bit more used to my load," said Peter, hitching it up high. "But goodness – how I wish I could put it down just for a minute!"

"Look – there's a river!" said Anna, pointing to where a line of blue appeared. "How shall we cross that?"

"Oh, I dare say there's a bridge," said Patience. "Come on!"

But when they got to the river, there was no bridge to be seen – and no boat either! The grown-ups came along and stared at the swift-running river.

"We've got to cross it," said Mr. Scornful. "It lies between us and that hill."

A shepherd was not far off, minding sheep that grazed on the moors around. Mr. Scornful hailed him.

"Is this river dangerous?"

"Of course!" said the shepherd. "Can't you see how swift-running it is? Many a man has been drowned in it through trying to cross just here."

"Oh, my!" said Gracie, don't let's try to cross it! For goodness' sake let's go back."

"Yes, let's said Mr. Fearful at once. "I'm not going to be drowned."

"What cowards you are!" said Mr. Scornful. "It may be swift-running – but it doesn't look very deep. I'm going to try wading across."

He stepped into it – but the swift current caught hold of him and swept him off his feet at once. His heavy burden prevented him from swimming, and if he had not caught hold of a log that was sailing down just then, he would most certainly have been drowned. The others screamed in fright. Peter held out his hand to him and helped him to the bank again.

"This is terrible!" said Mr. Scornful, wringing out his wet clothes. "What a dangerous river! What's it called, shepherd?"

"It is the River Trouble," said the shepherd. "Farther up there are stepping-stones, just by the Ford of Determination. You may get across there, if the river isn't running too high."

"We'd better go and see," said Mr. Scornful. So they set off up the river, in the direction to which the shepherd had pointed. Mr. Fearful hung on to Mr. Scornful's arm and poured out all kinds of objections.

"Don't let's try to get across! You can see the river is running high! Even if we get across we shall be wet through. And suppose I fall in? Who's going to get me out? Let's go back to the city. Even if we have to carry these burdens, never mind. We may get used to them!"

"Yes, let's go back," said Dick Cowardly. "The very thought of stepping-stones makes me shiver."

"I'm tired of this journey already," said Gracie. "I wish I'd never set out."

"You're a pack of miseries," said Mr. Scornful, in his sneering voice. "Not one of you has any sense! Why, even the children are more sensible than you!"

They came at last to the ford. Here the river ran much shallower, and big stones were set out across it that would take a traveller to the other side, provided he was bold and careful. The children stood and gazed at the stones, wondering if they could jump from one to the other with their short legs.

"Well, if any one thinks I'm going to try doing circus tricks across those stones, they're mistaken!" said Mr. Fearful, in a firm voice. "Because I'm not."

"Well, I am!" said Peter, suddenly, making up his mind to do his best, and to help Anna and Patience across too. "They don't look too difficult, if you take them one at a time!"

ONCE THEY HAD MADE UP THEIR MINDS TO CROSS THE SWIFT
RIVER, IT DID NOT SEEM QUITE SO DREADFUL

"I can't, I can't!" wailed Mr. Fearful, going quite pale at the thought. Mr. Scornful gave him a hard push that nearly sent him into the river.

"If you don't cross the River Trouble at the Ford of Determination, there's no other way of getting to the other bank," he said roughly. "You always were a poor thing, brother. I shall not help you. I shall give my hand to our cousin, Miss Simple. She at least doesn't wail or grumble!"

Mr. Scornful stepped on to the first stone and held out his hand to Miss Simple. She gave him a bright smile and jumped beside him.

"I must just make up my mind to be brave!" she said.

"That's what you two girls have got to do, too," said Peter, taking hold of his sisters' hands. "Now then – face up to it – set your teeth – and over the River Trouble we'll go and reach the other side!"

"Let me go with you," said Dick Cowardly. "You're such a brave boy. It does me good to follow you. Come on, Gracie. The stones are not as slippery as you might think."

The children found it difficult to jump from one stepping-stone to another – and yet not so difficult as they had feared. Once they had made up their minds to cross the swift river, it did not seem quite so dreadful. But to poor Mr. Fearful it was simply terrible. He stood on the bank moaning and groaning, quite unable to put his foot on the first stepping-stone!

"Isn't he awful?" said Peter to Anna, as they stood on a big flat stone in the middle of the river. "I do feel ashamed of him! Honestly, he makes me feel quite nervous if I listen to him."

"Well, don't then," said Anna. "Come on. The next stone is a bit of a jump. Gracious, I'm wet. My feet are soaked. Look how the river splashes over that next stone. You'll have to go first, and then help us, Peter."

At last all the little company except Mr. Fearful were safely on the opposite side of the River Trouble. They felt pleased with themselves. "We tackled that well," said Mr. Scornful. "Ah, well – I always say that the best way to tackle trouble is to make up your mind to face it with courage and determination! It's never so bad then!"

"Wait for me! Wait for me! Brother, come back and help me across!" wailed poor Mr. Fearful. Mr. Scornful curled up his lip.

"What a poor creature he is! And to think he is my brother too! Well – *I'm* not going to waste my time in helping him!"

"But oughtn't you to try?" said Peter, in surprise. "We can't leave him behind."

"Oh, *can't* we!" said Mr. Scornful. "Well, that's where you are mistaken. We *can* leave him behind – and we will! He makes me tired with all his wails and moans. Come along!"

So once again the little company set out – but this time there were only nine. Mr. Fearful had been left behind. He wept bitterly as he saw the others going off towards the hill in the distance. But he was much too afraid to go across the river by himself. The last that the children saw of him was a bowed figure in the distance, trudging all the way back to the City of Turmoil with his burden on his back.

"Well, it didn't take much to send him home again," said Peter. "How awful to be afraid of things, like that!"

"I almost was," said Dick Cowardly. "If I hadn't kept close to you, I'd never have got across either."

"We'll have to hurry," said Mr. Scornful, looking at the sun, which was now getting rather low in the sky. "We must find shelter for the night, for we don't want to sleep out here in the open. There might be robbers or wild beasts around."

"Oh, my goodness!" said Miss Simple, looking all round her for thieves or bears. "Don't say things like that! It makes my hair stand up on end!"

Down into a valley went the nine travellers, tired and hot. Mr. Scornful looked all about for some kind of shelter. He knew that they could not climb the hill that day, although by now they were quite near to it.

"Ah! There's a cottage!" said Miss Simple, in delight. "We can stay there for the night – and maybe they will give us supper! Come along – we'll go and knock at the door.

And off to the little cottage they went. Peter banged at the door, and every one waited behind him. Who lived there, and what kind of a welcome would they get?

CHAPTER FOUR

A NIGHT IN KINDLY'S COTTAGE. MR. SCORNFUL HAS A BAD TIME. MRS. DALLY AND MR. DOUBT.

A tall old man opened the door. He was a peasant, and had a ruddy, friendly face. He seemed surprised to see such a company.

"Old fellow, can you give us shelter for the night?" asked

Mr. Scornful, pushing his way forward. "A barn will do for the children. We want food too."

"I can give you bread and milk," said the peasant. "And a little cheese between you. There is room in the kitchen for the children – and you grown-ups must do with the old barn."

"I can pay well," said Mr. Scornful, going into the cottage and looking round. "I want something better than bread, milk, and cheese. And as for sleeping on a barn floor, that's a thing I'd never do. All very well for poor folk – but I'm the rich Mr. Scornful. I must have the best."

"My name is Kindly," said the old peasant, his bright blue eyes shining in the evening sunlight. "I have nothing to offer you but simple food. And I say again that these tired children must have my kitchen. The barn must do for you others."

"I'm quite willing," said Miss Simple. "I don't mind anything so long as I'm happy. I'll help you to get the meal, Mr. Kindly."

But Mr. Scornful was hungry, and he looked sneeringly at the brown loaf, creamy milk, and yellow cheese which was all that Kindly had to offer. He went outside and looked at the barn.

He came back to the cottage and called to the peasant, who was getting some bedding from the loft, to put down in the kitchen for the tired children.

"Hie! Isn't there anywhere else near here where we can get better food? And more comfortable shelter?"

"Well, Mr. Wealthy lives in that big house on the hillside there," said Kindly. "He has plenty of rich food, and silk sheets on all his beds. Pink sheets for the pink room, blue for the blue room – oh, marvellous! But he's rather mean, so he might not welcome you. And you'd have to be careful not to go near his watch-dogs."

"Well, I'm going along there," said Mr. Scornful at once. "I may know him. I'm pretty rich myself. Sarah Simple, you'd better come with me – and you, too, Dick and Gracie. The children will be all right here."

But the others were too tired to move. The children sat eating the bread and milk, and looked longingly at the bedding that the peasant was spreading on the floor for them. Mr. Scornful smiled his jeering smile and stepped out of the door.

"Well, I'm off to a good meal and a comfortable bed!" he said. "See you in the morning. Good-bye!"

The children curled themselves up on the bedding spread on the floor, and in a moment or two were sound asleep. Kindly took the three grown-ups to his barn, and showed them where they could lie in the soft hay. It smelt sweet and good. The old peasant lay down with them, for he had given the five children all his bedding. It was not long before they were all sound asleep.

In the morning the sun streamed into the kitchen and the barn. The children and the grown-ups ate porridge cooked by Kindly. Miss Simple helped him, chattering all the time.

"You know, we're on our way to the Land of Far-Beyond, to get rid of these dreadful burdens. We've got to climb up that hill. I hope it won't be very difficult."

"You will get a sight of the Land of Far-Beyond at the top," said Kindly. "The Guide lives there, in his small house. He will help you, and tell you the way to go. When will you set out? You must not start late, or you will not get up to the top before nightfall. I will give you food for the way."

"We must wait for Mr. Scornful," said Miss Simple. "I expect he has overslept this morning! No doubt he had a big supper, and a soft bed last night – and did not wake with the sun as we did."

"Look – who's this coming?" said Peter, suddenly. He had caught sight of a strange figure coming slowly up to the cottage. It was a man. His hair was wild, his eyes were bloodshot, his hands were bleeding. His clothes were torn and ragged. But on his back was the same kind of burden as the others carried.

Kindly looked hard at the man coming slowly along. "Why, it's the man who didn't want to stay here last night!" he said, in surprise. "What *can* have happened to him?"

"It's Mr. Scornful!" cried Peter. "Goodness me – how awful he looks! Mr. Scornful, whatever has happend to you? We've been imagining you having rich food and sleeping between silk sheets!"

"I haven't had a bite of food or a wink of sleep," said Mr. Scornful, wearily. "First of all I lost my way. Then I fell into a tangle of thorns. At last I came to Mr. Wealthy's house, and because I looked dirty, and my clothes were torn by the thorns, and because I carried this load on my back, his servants would not let me in."

"Well, what did you do then?" asked Anna.

"I shouted at the top of my voice," said Mr. Scornful. "I hoped that Mr. Wealthy might hear me and come to see what the matter was. Then I thought he would know me, and let me in. But the servants beat me and set two dogs on me. I tried to find my way back here, but it was dark. When the sun rose I saw the cottage in the distance – and here I am."

"Well, you scorned my poor food and my shelter last night,"

"FIRST OF ALL I LOST MY WAY, THEN I FELL INTO A TANGLE
OF THORNS"

said Kindly, in his pleasant voice. "But you are welcome to it still. Better to have simple fare in a kindly house, than seek for better things in a place where there is no welcome. Come in and rest awhile."

Poor Mr. Scornful was only too glad to come in and eat the food he had scorned the night before. Then he lay down on some hay in the barn and fell fast asleep.

"He does not really need silk sheets!" laughed Miss Simple. "Now what are we to do? He may sleep for hours! We can't wait for him."

"Better start off," said Kindly. "I'll tell him the way you've gone. Now listen to me carefully, or you may get into difficulties."

Every one stood round, listening to the blue-eyed peasant. "Take that path," he said, pointing with his staff. "It is steep, but it will bring you to the Guide's hut before nightfall. Do not take any easier way, for if you do, you may get lost, and it is not pleasant to be out on the hillside in the dark."

"Shall we meet any one?" asked Peter. "Does any one else live on the hill?"

"Yes. Dally lives there, in a pleasant cottage," said Kindly. "Take no notice of her. She is an old gossip, and will keep you listening to her until she makes you late. And some one else may try to keep you, too. It is the old man, Mr. Doubt, who worries many travellers in this life. Take no notice of either of them."

"All right," said Peter. "We'll go now. I'm impatient to get on! I hope Mr. Scornful won't be long. He's a funny sort of fellow, always turning up his nose at everything, and thinking we're all stupid – but still, he's a sort of leader, and we shall miss him."

The little company set off again. The shepherd showed them how to cut sticks from the hazel hedge, and these were a great help to every one as they began to climb the steep path that led up the hill. The sun shone down hotly again, and every one panted, for their burdens seemed twice as heavy going uphill.

"How I wish we could rest a bit!" sighed Gracie Grumble. "This is a much worse journey than I expected. I wouldn't have set out if I'd known what I was going to go through."

"Well, nothing very dreadful has happened," said Patience.

"But think what *might* have happened!" said Dick Cowardly, shuddering. "We might have fallen in the River Trouble! We might never have found Kindly's cottage, and have had to spend the night as Mr. Scornful did. We might . . ."

"Be quiet!" said Miss Simple. "You make me feel afraid. Oh, isn't this sun hot? I do wish we could rest."

"There's a nice little cottage over there," said Anna. "I wonder if we could get a drink of water there."

"We'll go and see," said Peter, and he set off towards it. An old dame with a rather silly little face opened her door to him.

"Of course you can have a drink!" she said. "I'll get a jug of water for you – ice-cold from the spring! Come and rest for a while in my little garden and tell me all your news. You shall see my three new kittens – and I've a dear little kid you'll love to play with."

"Well, we can't stop," said Peter. "But we *would* like a drink."

So the old dame gave them all cups of cold water and chattered to them as they sat drinking. It was pleasant in the little garden. A cool breeze blew, and the view was lovely.

"Let's stay a while," said Gracie Grumble. "I'm so tired."

"We mustn't be too long," said Patience, stretching herself out on the grass.

"Oh, stay as long as you like," said the old woman, and she began to tell them all sorts of things, and to beg them to tell her their news.

Miss Simple poured out the tale of their adventures. Anna fell asleep. Dick Cowardly wandered round the garden, picking raspberries. It was all very pleasant.

"I really think we'd better go," said Peter, suddenly. "The sun is disappearing down the other side of the hill already. Good-bye, old woman. What is your name?"

"Mrs. Dally," said the old dame. Peter stared in dismay

"We were warned against her!" he said in a low voice to the others. "Hurry! She has taken up our time and made us laze away half the day. We'll never be at the Guide's before nightfall if we don't hurry."

"Oh, let's stay and have a cup of tea," begged Gracie Grumble. "Mrs. Dally would love us to, I'm sure."

But although Mrs. Dally begged them all to have tea with her, Peter would not hear of it. He hurried the children up the hill-path, leaving the others to follow.

"There's no sign of Mr. Scornful yet," he said, looking down the hill. "I hope he catches us up soon. We have wasted plenty of time at Mrs. Dally's, so maybe he'll soon be with us."

The path was very steep just there. Gracie Grumble panted and groaned, and when they came to where the way forked, and the two paths went either side of the hill, one much easier than the other, Gracie wanted to go the less steep way.

"Well, do what you please," said Dick Cowardly. "I'll go with you, if you like."

So the two parted company with the others, and planned to meet them at the cottage of the Guide at the top of the hill. The other six toiled on up the hill.

It was terribly steep. Stones rolled down beneath their feet. Anna slipped and fell and had to be hauled up again by Peter. Her knees were bleeding.

Then Patience got her hands scratched by a bush, and began to cry. "I don't like this hill," she wept. "I want to go back home!"

"Cheer up," said Peter. "Look – there's somebody's house just here. We'll go in and bathe your hands and Anna's knees. Come along!"

So along to the cottage they went. Mr. Doubt lived there, and he opened the door to them at once.

"Dear, dear!" he said, when he saw the hurt children. "Have you been trying to climb this awful hill? Now whatever did you do that for? It isn't worth it! The view at the top is nearly always hidden in mist. Come along in."

The five children and Sarah Simple went into the cottage. Mr. Doubt, who was a shifty-looking fellow with curious eyes, got some warm water to bathe Anna's knees and Patience's hands.

"Aren't his eyes funny!" whispered Anna. "One is blue and the other is brown."

"How glad I am we saw this place," said Miss Simple, sitting down in a chair with a sigh. "I'm very tired, and glad of a rest. Thank goodness we came here!"

But it wasn't a good thing at all, as it turned out!

CHAPTER FIVE

MISS SIMPLE IS VANQUISHED BY MR. DOUBT. A NIGHT ON THE HILLSIDE. RESCUE OF DICK COWARDLY AND GRACIE GRUMBLE

"My name is Henry Doubt," said their host, as he helped Peter to sponge Anna's knees. "I have to live up here on this hill for the sake of my health. But it is an awful place. It is terribly steep towards the top, and the country on the other side is dreary and desolate. I can't imagine why you are all travelling up here."

"We're going to the Land of Far-Beyond," said Peter. "Don't you see these dreadful burdens on our backs? We can get rid of them there."

"How do you know?" asked Mr. Doubt. "Why do you need to travel from home to get rid of them? You could just as easily rid yourselves of them there as travel miles away over difficult country."

"Ah, but they are not ordinary loads," said Anna. "A man called Wanderer said they were the burdens of wrong that lay in our hearts – and he gave them shape, and made these burdens appear on our backs. They are part of us. We can't get rid of them unless we leave the wicked City of Turmoil and go to the City of Happiness."

"Don't you believe it!" said Mr. Doubt. "Good gracious, what a silly tale! Those burdens won't disappear in the City of Happiness. Why should they?"

"I don't know," said Peter. "I just believed Wanderer when he said they would."

"Don't you really think they will?" asked Miss Simple, anxiously. "I really don't want to waste weeks of my time travelling through unknown and dangerous country in order to get rid of something that will never go. I might just as well be at home."

"Just as well," said Henry Doubt, sponging Patience's hands. "A pretty little person like you shouldn't have to run into danger. Goodness me, when I think of the wild animals about . . ."

"Oh!" squealed Sarah Simple, in fright.

"And the giant's castle," went on Mr. Doubt, his curious eyes gleaming as he looked at Miss Simple and the frightened children.

"Oh, my, oh, my!" moaned poor Miss Simple.

"And the Tunnel of Disgust," said Mr. Doubt, quite enjoying himself.

"Worse and worse!" said Miss Simple, beginning to weep. "I can't bear it. It hardly seems worth while running into all these dreadful things for the sake of getting rid of a burden I am really getting quite used to."

"Of course it isn't worth it," said Mr. Doubt. "You'd far better go back, all of you."

"Well, really I think I will," said Miss Simple, looking at the children. "Let's travel back down the hill to Kindly's, children – and then go home. After all, there's only you and me left now. Mr. Scornful won't join us again, I'm sure – and Dick Fearful

SO ALONG TO THE COTTAGE THEY WENT. MR. DOUBT LIVED
THERE, AND HE OPENED THE DOOR TO THEM AT ONCE

and Gracie Grumble may get lost. I don't want to have to go on alone with you poor children. I'd better take you back."

But the children did not want to go back. They did not believe all that Mr. Doubt said. After all, Wanderer had said it would be worth while going to the City of Happiness – and now that they had left behind the City of Turmoil, and had come out into the clean, wind-swept, sun-warmed countryside, they had no wish to return to that unclean, smelly, selfish town.

But Miss Simple had really believed all that Mr. Doubt had said. She got up and shook out her skirts. "Well, I'm going back," she said. "You children had better wait for a while and see if the others join you. I wouldn't advise you to go on alone."

She nodded to them and then went outside. The children watched her through the open door. She took the path that led down the hill. Peter was sad to see her go.

"She wasn't very clever; she was really rather stupid." he said. "But she was quite nice and kind. I'm sorry she's gone back. That's two people we've lost now – Mr. Fearful and Miss Simple."

"You'd better go home too," said Mr. Doubt. "You really had. It's not safe for children to wander about here alone. My dear boy, take the girls back home, you've no right to let them run into danger."

"Oh, dear," said Peter, half-convinced that he ought to take the girls back, at any rate. "I simply don't know what to do!"

At that moment there came the sound of footsteps, and who should come hastening up the path but Mr. Scornful, red in the face, and panting hard. He had awakened late, and had at once set out after the others. He had not stopped at Mrs. Dally's as they had, so he had been able to catch them up.

"What's all this about Sarah Simple going off home?" he said, as soon as he saw the others. "I've just met her, and she simply refuses to go on!"

"Well, sir, she's very wise," said Henry Doubt. "I've been telling her it's not worth it."

"So *you* put stupid ideas into her head, did you?" said Mr. Scornful, angrily. "She's a nice, simple, trusting little woman, and wanted to get rid of her burden just as much as we did. And now you've managed to make her change her mind. Well, well – I'll go on with the children. You won't change *my* mind, I can tell you."

The children were really pleased to see Mr. Scornful again. He was a sneering, selfish kind of man, but, at any rate, he did know his own mind and, wasn't afraid of anything. So they left

33

Mr. Doubt's house and set out with Mr. Scornful quite willingly. They told him that Gracie Grumble and Dick Cowardly had taken another path and were to meet them at the top of the hill.

"Ha! I expect they've tried to take an easier way," said Mr. Scornful. "I know old Dick – he can't face hardships and always tries to go round them instead of facing up to them! Well – goodness knows if they'll meet us or not. Come along. We've no time to waste. It's getting dark now."

The sun had quite disappeared over the hill and the valley below was dark with night-mist. The children toiled upwards, glad of their stout hazel staffs to help them.

A mist swirled down over them and they shivered, for it was damp. Mr. Scornful stopped and looked around "Now this is tiresome," he said. "This mist hides the way. We'd better be careful or we'll miss the path."

After a while there seemed to be no path to follow. The five children had to scramble along as best they could. Night came down, and the thick mist hid the stars above. It was very frightening.

"Couldn't we find a cave or some kind of shelter?" called Peter to Mr. Scornful. "We'll roll down the hill if we miss our footing – and we simply can't see where we're walking."

"We'll look for one," said Mr. Scornful. "I'm afraid we shan't reach the top of the hill to-night."

By great good luck the five children came to a kind of shallow cave, and went inside. The mist did not seem to penetrate there, and it was warmer. They huddled together.

"Couldn't we light a fire?" asked Peter. "I'm so hungry and cold. We've nothing to eat – but at least a fire would be cheerful."

Mr. Scornful, Peter, and John hunted for twigs and bits of wood. They soon had a fire going at the entrance to the cave, and it made a warm and cheerful blaze.

"It will keep off wild animals, anyway," said Lily.

They all cuddled together – and suddenly, after about an hour, Peter lifted his head. He had heard something.

It sounded like a growl or groan. Could it be some wild animal on the hunt? He looked towards Mr. Scornful, who was lying on the ground asleep. He called to him.

"Mr. Scornful! I can hear something. Do you think it's a wild animal?"

"Of course not, boy! Don't be such a silly," said Mr. Scornful, in his sneering voice, and promptly went to sleep again.

Peter watched and listened. He heard a rustling sound. He

heard what sounded like growls and groans again. He began to tremble. It could be nothing but a wild animal. Surely a little fire would not keep it away. Suppose it leapt over the flames and came into the cave?

Then he saw something. The Something came crawling up the hill towards the fire, and it made a noise as it came. Peter hit Mr. Scornful on the shoulder to wake him, and picked up his stick.

Mr. Scornful woke with a jump. "Look! There's something coming!" cried Peter, and threw his stick at whatever is was. A shout of pain came from the Something.

"Don't! You've hit me! Oh, save me, whoever you are!"

"My goodness, it's Dick Cowardly!" cried Peter in astonishment. Every one was awake now, and they crowded to the entrance of the cave. On the other side of the fire lay poor Dick Cowardly, his clothes torn and his face pale. He had been crawling up the hillside towards the glow of the fire.

"Where's Gracie?" demanded Mr. Scornful.

"She's down there, in that hollow," said Dick Cowardly, pointing feebly downwards. "I saw this light and came for help. We took a path that really seemed much easier than the other – but it led to a steep precipice, and we both fell over. We lay in the gully below, bruised and hurt, until I saw the light of your fire, and somehow made my way up the steep hillside to it. Then you threw something at me and hit me."

"I'm sorry," said Peter. "We'd better go and find Miss Grumble. Shall we take a torch from the fire, Mr. Scornful?"

So, armed with three flaring torches, Peter, John, and Mr. Scornful went to look for the gully where Dick Cowardly said that Gracie was lying. He would not go with them because he was to frightened of falling again.

They found poor Grace. She could walk, but she was so terribly sorry for herself that she could do nothing but weep and wail all the way up the hill. The others were sorry for her, but they couldn't help feeling impatient. After all, she had brought her trouble on herself, and she might at least have been grateful to her rescuers!

"If only we hadn't waited so long at Mrs. Dally's, and listened to Mr. Doubt!" said Patience. "We might have been at the top of the hill by now. I am sure that if we could have got to the Guide's hut we should have been quite all right. This is a dreadful night. I'm cold again now, and so wide awake that I'll not be able to go to sleep any more."

"Oh, dear! I expect the Guide's cottage will be miles away," sighed Gracie Grumble. "We'll have to climb for ages to-morrow, and I'm so bruised and tired."

Nobody went to sleep again that night. They tried to keep up the fire, but it went out. The mist of the early morning came into the cave and made them shiver. Then at last the sun rose, and its rays warmed the hill. The children stretched out their hands to it.

"Now come along," said Mr. Scornful, getting up from his cold seat on the ground. "Even if we have to climb for miles, we must set our teeth and do it. On to the top of the hill!"

CHAPTER SIX

THE GUIDE'S COTTAGE. GREED AND SPITE. THE FIERCE DOGS AND
DAME DREAD. THE YOUTH CALLED BOLD. DAME FRIENDLY

A pleasant surprise awaited every one. When they left the little cave in which they had spent the night the mist blew away suddenly. The children gave loud cries of surprise and joy.

"Why, we're almost at the top of the hill! Look! Look!"

"Another ten minutes' climb and we'll be there!"

"How marvellous! We must have climbed higher in the night than we guessed!"

"And see – there is a hut!" cried Peter. "It must be the Guide's. Why, we were so near that if we had shouted for help he would have heard us and come! Hurry, hurry! Maybe he will give us breakfast."

Even Gracie Grumble forgot to sigh and moan, and hastened up the little winding path, half-forgetting the heaviness of her burden. The little hut looked gay and welcoming in the early morning sun. It was built of stone that glinted and shone, and the diamond-paned windows gleamed gold where the sun's rays caught them. Smoke rose from the chimneys, and somebody was singing a song beyond the house.

"That must be the Guide," said Peter, and he gave a shout. An answering cry came from behind the house and some one came hurrying round. At first the children thought that it must be Wanderer again, for this man was dressed exactly the same, and he had the same happy, shining look in his eyes and on his face. Then they saw that he was a little different, not so tall, and with a more peaceful look in his eyes than the Wanderer had had. He came to greet them.

"I thought at first you were the Wanderer," said Anna, in surprise.

"He is my brother," said the Guide, smiling at her. "We are very alike. How tired and hungry you all look. You must come and rest – and feast your eyes on my view!"

Then, for the first time, the travellers saw the view over the other side of the hill, towards the west. Their eyes strained to a gleaming country far beyond – a country whose great towers glittered in the sun – a land that seemed magical and enchanted, full of mystery and beauty.

"You can see the City of Happiness from here," said the Guide. "Those are its towers."

"Are all the people happy there?" asked Patience. "Have they shining faces like you and Wanderer?"

"Of course," said the Guide. "Their hearts are at peace because there is nothing but kindliness and love there. Those things shine out from any one's eyes. I hope they will shine from yours when you reach there. If they do not you will not be allowed to stay!"

"Oh," said Anna, looking round at the others to see if any of them had shining eyes and happy faces. But not one of them had. They all looked tired and strained, and on the faces of the grown-ups were ugly lines and wrinkles, put there by discontent and selfishness.

Every one stood gazing at the Land of Far-Beyond. Then they saw what lay between! An ugly desolate country stretched between the hill and the far-off land. Hills reared up their heads, marshes lay wreathed in mists, swift rivers raced along, and rocky stretches were spread for miles.

"So that is the country we must cross," said Peter. "I don't like it. It will be hard."

"It is always hard to win anything that is really worth while," said the Guide. He took them into a sunny living-room and set out food on the table there.

Every one was terribly hungry. Even Mr. Scornful did not turn up his nose this time! He fell to with as much appetite as any one else. Dick Cowardly and Gracie Grumble had had their bruises soothed with ointments, and they were feeling much happier.

"I wish Miss Simple was here," said Peter. "It seems funny without her."

"It was a pity she went to Mr. Doubt's," said Mr. Scornful.

HORACE KNOWLES....

THEN, FOR THE FIRST TIME, THE TRAVELLERS SAW THE VIEW
OVER THE OTHER SIDE OF THE HILL

38

"She always believed everything she was told, poor creature. Never used her brain! Ah, well – I suppose she's half-way back to the City of Turmoil now. It's funny – I didn't at all mind living there but now when I think of it, I hate the idea."

"You must all rest after your meal," said the Guide. "Then I will tell you the best way to go to the Land of Far-Beyond, and give you a map to show you the way."

"Thank you," said Mr. Scornful, stretching himself and yawning. "Well, I must say I could do with a good nap after our wakeful night. It's a mercy we haven't all got chills!"

Some of the company rested out in the sunny garden. Gracie Grumble lay on the Guide's bed. Mr. Scornful stretched himself out in the only comfortable chair in the hut. Every one slept soundly on the hill-top, feeling the cool breeze blowing round and seeing the view whenever they opened sleepy eyes.

Peter and the others turned themselves about to see the City of Turmoil, that lay on the other side of the hill, to the east. It seemed dreadful, after the shining city that lay to the west. Heavy clouds hung over it, and the city looked dark, smoky, and ugly. Peter shivered.

"Fancy! We lived in that dark, ugly place," he said. "And yet we were so used to it that we never noticed how ugly it was."

"I hope we never go back," said Anna, and Patience agreed.

Later on in the morning the Guide told them the way they must go. "You must climb down this hill," he said, "and keep to the narrow way that will lead you safely over the rough country to the west. You will meet many of the people who live between here and Far-Beyond, but do not be tempted to turn aside with them. And do not be afraid of any dangers or difficulties you come to. Face them and they will grow small – run away and they will come after you!"

He turned to Mr. Scornful. "You, sir, will have to be careful to be content with simple things and not to go chasing riches or power. You must not scorn others for stupidity or kindliness – if you do, you will lose your way and never reach the City of Happiness."

"Now don't try to teach me things I've heard since I was in the cradle!" said Mr. Scornful, impatiently. "I know what's what! I know that there isn't much happiness without money and power."

"I am happy, and I have neither," said the Guide, his eyes gleaming as he looked at Mr. Scornful. "Well, you must go your own way and learn your own lessons." He turned to the children again. "Keep together, and help one another," he said. "As long as you are on the narrow way, you are safe, and nothing can harm you. See that you do not stray from it."

"Very well," said Peter, and he took up his staff. "We'd better start right away. Do you think, sir, that we might take a little food with us?"

"Of course," said the Guide, and he began to pack up bread and cheese, and some fruit to quench their thirst on the way. "I will take you down the hill myself."

They all set off together. It was almost as tiring going down the hill as up!

"My feet will keep wanting to run down, and I daren't let them in case I wouldn't be able to stop!" said Anna.

The Guide took them right down to the bottom of the hill. It was a good thing he did, for the way was very overgrown, and the little company might easily have missed it if they had gone by themselves. At the foot the Guide said good-bye, and the children waved to him as they set off along the narrow, winding path he had pointed out to them.

"Well, it seems quite easy," said Patience, as they all walked along in single file. "If all we have to do is to walk along like this, it shouldn't be more than a day or two before we reach the Land of Far-Beyond. Didn't it look lovely from the top of the hill?"

"We can't see it from here, now that we are down in the valley," said Peter. "What a pity! It would have helped us along if we had been able to look up and see it!"

For an hour or two the eight people trudged along in the morning sun. It was now rising high, and would soon be at its greatest height in the sky. The children panted with the heat.

"Let's eat some of our fruit," said Anna. "I'm so thirsty."

They sat down in the shade of a big tree. As they undid the packets of fruit and bread, Anna caught sight of the heads of two children peeping round a tree not far off.

"Who are they?" she said, in wonder. "What horrid faces they've got!"

Every one looked as the two children came near. One was very fat, and his little piggy eyes were half-buried in the folds of his cheeks. The other had a mean, spiteful face, and he licked his lips as he saw the food that the little group were eating.

"Give us some," said the fat boy, whose name was Greed.

The other boy, who was called Spiteful, made a grab at John's fruit. John wasn't in time to save it and the boy crammed most of it into his mouth at once. He grinned spitefully at the angry boy, and gave him a hard pinch before running off.

The other boy snatched up a bag in which was some cheese that the Guide had given the travellers. He crammed his mouth full too, and then, as Mr. Scornful, John and Peter rose to their feet in anger, he took to his heels and raced away. Peter tore after the two boys. He was a fast runner, and was not going to let the two mean boys go free without a punishment.

"Come back!" shouted Mr. Scornful. "You will lose us if you go too far!"

"Peter! You know what the Guide said – we weren't to leave the path!" cried Anna. So Peter came back annoyed that Greed and Spite had got away.

"I'll jolly well look out for them and go for them if they come back again," he said, fiercely.

"I expect we shall meet all kinds of queer folk on our way," said Dick Cowardly. "The Guide said we should."

"And do you remember what Mr. Doubt said?" said Anna. "He told us about the giant's castle – and the Tunnel of Disgust. There must be heaps of strange things in this desolate country."

They set off again and walked until the sun was half-way down the sky. Then they felt very tired, for their burdens always seemed heaviest towards the end of the day.

"Where do you think we can pass the night?" asked Patience. "Did the Guide tell you?"

"He marked a place on the map he gave me," said Mr. Scornful, unrolling the big map. "Yes – here it is – a house called Restful, owned by a Dame Friendly. It should be quite near here."

Every one felt glad. They began to look around for the house. After a while John spied it, half-hidden among some trees.

"There it is!" he said. "It looks a nice welcoming sort of place too – there are lights in the windows already, although it is not really dark."

As they drew near the house, some dogs set up a great barking, and the children saw that four fierce dogs were roaming to and fro in the garden. Every one halted.

"I don't like the look of those," said Patience, trembling. "Look at their teeth!"

"I shouldn't think that this can be Dame Friendly's house, if she keeps fierce dogs like that," said Anna.

"I don't dare to open the gate," said Dick Cowardly. "I simply don't dare!"

"Well, I got so pulled about by dogs the night before last that I don't feel inclined to face them either," said Mr. Scornful. "I think we'd better go on."

"Well – it really *does* look as if this should be the house," said Peter, looking at the map. "Shall I go up to the door and ask? Maybe if I said "Good dog, good dog!" they wouldn't bite me."

An old woman covered in a dirty grey cloak came up the way beside them, tap-tapping with her stick. She stopped and looked at the company.

"I am Dame Dread," she said. "Don't you go near those dogs. Come with me, and I'll hide you before they come leaping over the wall!"

Dick Cowardly went over to Dame Dread at once. "I'll go with you," he said, his teeth chattering. "Do you live near here? Could you put me up for the night?"

"Well, I'm not very pleasant company," said Dame Dread, grinning at Dick, and showing her toothless gums. "But if you like to hide in my cellar, you're welcome."

Poor Dick Cowardly went off with Dame Dread. "I wouldn't have gone with *her*!" said Lily. "What a horrid old woman she looked!"

"Well, we're no better off than we were," said Gracie Grumble, looking after Dick as if she had half a mind to follow him. "I don't know which would be the better thing to do – sleep in that grey old dame's cellar all night – or face being bitten by the dogs!"

A youth came up the path, whistling. He carried a basket of washing on his shoulder. He went up to the gate and opened it.

"Hie, you! Mind those dogs!" cried Peter.

The youth, whose name was Bold, grinned back at Peter. "Come and look!" he cried. "They are all on long chains! They can't get at you!"

And sure enough he was right! The fierce dogs each had long chains that prevented them from reaching the path that led up to the house. Bold went up to the door and delivered his washing. Mr. Scornful looked ashamed of himself. He went up the path too, followed by Gracie and the children, whilst the dogs all barked madly.

"Lie down, lie down!" cried a voice, and the children saw a kindly faced woman at the door. Surely it must be Dame Friendly! It was, and a nicer person could surely never be found anywhere. What a fuss she made of the children! How she laughed when they told her they had been so frightened of her dogs!

"Bless us all, I keep them to frighten away robbers and thieves, not harmless folk like you!" she said. "Now see, I've meat-pies hot in the oven, and cocoa boiling in the pot. Help yourselves! Put down your burdens for a while."

But that no one could do, much as they wanted to. It was quite impossible. They sat and ate, wondering how poor Dick Cowardly was getting on.

In the morning they met him again on the road. He was grey with fear, for he was quite certain that all the others had been eaten by the dogs! He was amazed to see them walking along happily together, talking about the pleasant night they had had at Dame Friendly's.

"I spent the night in a damp dark cellar, listening for the dogs," he said. "Dame Dread told me the most awful stories about them – and about all the dangers on this road. I didn't sleep a wink. I just couldn't. I shivered and shook, and every time a beetle ran over my foot I yelled."

"Poor Dick Cowardly," said Peter. "You do fill yourself up with fears and frights, and you don't need to!"

"Now we've a good long way to go to-day," said Mr. Scornful, looking at his map. "If we travel fast, we should come to the House of Peace to-night. But we pass all kinds of queer places on the way! Look – that is the Wood of Deceit – and here is the Marsh of Dishonesty – with stepping-stones of Truth going through it. We don't go near it, really – our path keeps well to the north."

"Well, for goodness' sake let's all keep together," said Gracie Grumble, looking at Dick. "Don't go wandering off with dirty old dames, and sleeping in cellars that make you smell musty, Cousin Dick!"

CHAPTER SEVEN

THE WOOD OF DECEIT. THE HOUSE OF LIES. TRICKERY, BLUFF
AND GAMBLE. THE MARSH OF DISHONESTY. MR. STRAIGHT AND
THE STEPPING-STONES OF TRUTH

The travellers went along the path, and followed its winding ways. Lily and John lagged a little behind, and suddenly saw a bag lying by the wayside. They ran to it and picked it up. It was full of money!

"Oooh!" said Lily, putting her fingers in among the coins. "Look, John! What a lot of money!"

"Don't let's tell the others," said John at once. "They would only want to make us share. Let's say nothing."

"Well, we'll have to hide the money about us somewhere," said Lily, "or we shall be seen carrying the bag. Look – there's a wood nearby. We'll go among the trees and hide the money in our clothes. You can put some in your pockets and I can slip some into my stockings."

The two children slipped aside into the thick wood, and made their way to where the trees stood close together. They hurriedly emptied the bag of money and hid the coins about their clothes.

"Now we'll run and join the others," said John. "And mind you don't say a word about the money, Lily. It's ours, not theirs!"

But when they wanted to find their way out of the wood, they couldn't! The trees seemed to stand close together, and bar their way. The bushes were so prickly that it was hard to get round them.

They came to a little forlorn-looking hut and went inside to see if they could find some one to ask their way. But the door slammed to behind them and made them jump! They called to see if there was any one in the house, and some small dwarfs came running into the kitchen.

"Can you tell us the way to the narrow path?" asked John.

"Yes, if you pay us," said one of the dwarfs, an ugly little fellow with squinting eyes.

"We haven't any money," said John, at once.

"Then you can stay here, in the House of Lies, until you earn some money!" cried the dwarf. "We want servants. You shall be ours. Set to work and scrub the floor for us, and clean out the grates."

The two poor children were forced to set to work. All the dwarfs but one left the house. The one who was left prodded and pinched Lily and John to make them work more quickly.

"What are the burdens on your backs?" he asked.

"Nothing," said Lily. "We are travellers. Can't we carry our luggage on our backs?"

"That is not luggage," said the dwarf. "Ah, you are good servants for the House of Lies in the Wood of Deceit! You will work well for us. It's a good thing you had no money, or we would have set you free if you had paid us a small sum. Now you will have to do the work instead of me!"

He gave John such a push that the boy fell over his bucket,

BUT WHEN THEY WANTED TO FIND THEIR WAY OUT OF THE
WOOD, THEY COULDN'T! THE TREES SEEMED TO STAND CLOSE
TOGETHER, AND BAR THEIR WAY

and spilt the water. "Mop it up, mop it up!" cried the dwarf really enjoying himself.

"Listen, dwarf," said John, picking himself up. "We told a lie when we said we had no money. We have plenty."

"Where did you get it?" asked the dwarf, curiously.

"We found it in a bag lying by the wayside," said Lily. "We thought we wouldn't tell the others – so we hid the money about ourselves. Please let us go, dwarf, and we'll give you some."

As the children spoke the truth, the door slowly opened of itself, and John suddenly caught sight of it. The dwarf banged it shut. "That door always opens when any one tells the truth," he said. "Have you got a *lot* of money?"

"Yes," said John – and the door opened itself again. John caught hold of Lily's hand and the two children tore out of the House of Lies as fast as ever they could! The dwarf could not run after them, because he limped – so they were soon out of his sight.

"If only we could find our way!" said Lily, stopping and looking this way and that, hoping for a sight of the narrow path.

"I wish now we hadn't kept all the money for ourselves," said John. "It was mean and deceitful. If only we could join the others again I'd share every bit of it with them!"

Just at that moment the two children heard shouts. "That's Peter's voice!" cried John, and he yelled back.

Peter's voice came again. "John! Lily! Where are you?"

"Here! Here! We're coming!" shouted the two children, and they tore in the direction of Peter's voice. In a minute or two they came in sight of the narrow path – and how glad they were to see it again. They ran out of the Wood of Deceit, and came up to Peter.

"Wherever have you been?" asked Peter, indignantly. "We've been calling and searching for you for ages. It's too bad of you."

Lily was just going to make up some kind of excuse, when she remembered the horrid little House of Lies in which they had nearly been servants to the dwarfs. She told Peter the whole truth.

"We found some money and we didn't want to share it with you. So we ran into the wood to hide it in our clothes and we got lost. We came to a horrid little house called the House of Lies and some dwarfs made us be their servants. But we escaped, and here we are. And now we'll share every bit of the money with you and the others, Peter."

"Well, that's nice of you," said Peter, and he hurried them forward. "Mr. Scornful! Here they are! They got lost in the

Wood of Deceit, and were locked up in the House of Lies."

John and Lily shamefacedly found all the money they had hidden about themselves and gave it to the others. Mr. Scornful put a piece between his teeth and bit it hard. It broke in half.

"False money!" he said, in disgust, and threw it away. "It's no use. It's just false money made by thieves."

"And to think we had such a horrid adventure all because of something that wasn't worth even a penny," said Lily, beginning to weep.

'Come on, come on," said Mr. Scornful, who had no patience with tears. "Hurry! We've lost a lot of time looking for you two sillies."

They all hurried on again, sitting down at midday for a meal. Afterwards they had no time for a rest but went on their way, hoping to get to the House of Peace before nightfall.

They caught up three people on their way, who bowed to the little company, and began to talk.

"My name is Trickery," said the tallest of them, a man with bright red hair.

"Mine is Bluff," said his brother.

"And mine is Harriet Gamble," said the woman with them, a pretty creature with feverish eyes and flushed cheeks. "We are on our way to the House of Peace."

"So are we!" said Mr. Scornful. "We will travel together. It is good to be a large company in these desolate parts."

They journeyed on together. Trickery and Bluff were good company for they talked well, and made the others laugh continually. Soon they all came to a forking of the path, and to the children's surprise Trickery, Bluff and Harriet Gamble left the narrow path and went down the other one. Certainly it was a most inviting one, being broad and soft and spread with little flowers.

"Hie! You're going the wrong way!" called Mr. Scornful.

"No, we're not," said Trickery. Can't you see how rocky and rough the path gets, if you take the other direction. This leads to the House of Peace all right. We've often been this way."

"Have you really?" asked Gracie Grumble, who didn't at all like the look of the rough path nearby.

"Of course," said Trickery, and his bright eyes looked so honest and straight that every one believed him.

"There's been a fall of rocks or something along you path," said Bluff. "No one goes there now. We all take this short cut. You'd better come along with us, because if you don't you will

47

only find you can't get along the other path, and by the time you come back here we'll be gone."

"Well, we'll come with you now, then," said Anna, and she took Bluff's hand. She liked Bluff, with his merry smile and hearty manner, He had such a sure way with him too, that he made Anna feel safe. She was certain they would be all right with Bluff!

"It isn't very far before the path curves round and joins the other one," said Trickery, his red hair shining in the sun. "About ten minutes, I should think."

"Oh, well, if we shall so soon be back on the right path, we might as well go with you," said Mr. Scornful. So off they all went with Trickery, Bluff, and Miss Gamble.

Anna danced in front, calling to Bluff to race her. He ran after her – and suddenly poor Anna gave a dreadful scream. "I'm in a bog!" she cried. "My feet are sinking!"

The grass was very green where Anna was. This was the only sign that the ground had suddenly become marshy. Poor Anna was sinking fast in the boggy ground – and Trickery was sinking with her!

"Quick! We must pull Anna out!" cried Peter, and he ran to help. But alas, his feet too were caught in the marsh, and he began to flounder about, trying to get back to the hard ground.

Mr. Scornful had a rope round his burden to keep it from dragging on his shoulders too much. He undid it quickly, and threw it to Anna. She caught it, and began to pull herself back to safety. Trickery held on to her, and dragged her down with his weight.

"Let go!" shouted Peter, in a rage. "You are pulling my sister down!"

Anna and Trickery were at last got back to the hard ground. Anna was sobbing, and covered with slush. The others dried her as best they could.

Then Mr. Scornful turned to Trickery and his friends. "See what you nearly led us into!" he said, angrily. "That must be the Marsh of Dishonesty. By following you we were nearly caught in it."

"It has never been there before," said Bluff, turning his honest-seeming eyes on to Mr. Scornful. But they dropped before that man's hard gaze. Mr. Scornful had often been a rogue himself, and tricked others – he knew now that the three travellers were rogues too. He turned aside and called to the others.

48

"We must get back to the right path. Rocky as it looked, it will be better than falling into this marsh."

They set off back again, with Trickery, Bluff, and Harriet Gamble behind them. But they could not seem to find the way back, and it was not long before they found their feet sinking into squelchy ground. Anna was terrified after her experience and cried with fright.

Soon it seemed as if the marsh lay all around them. It smelt evil. Mists rose here and there from it. It was flat and horrible, with big tufts of rough-looking grass here and there.

"This is terrible," said Gracie Grumble. "Really terrible. We shall never get out! Whatever are we to do?"

"It looks as if there might be hard ground over there!" said Mr. Scornful, pointing. "Let's try to make our way there."

But it wasn't a bit of use. Every one began to sink down, and poor Mr. Scornful, with his heavy burden, sank right up to his knees, and found great difficulty in getting his feet out again. And, indeed, no sooner had he got them out than they sank down once more!

Night began to fall. The children were frightened, and called to the grown-ups. "Oh, do find a way out! We are so afraid."

"Isn't there any way through this horrible marsh?" Mr. Scornful asked Trickery, who was floundering about beside him. "Surely there must be some path."

"I've never heard of any, said Trickery sullenly.

"Mr. Scornful! Don't you remember that the map showed this marsh? It was called the Marsh of Dishonesty," said Gracie, suddenly. "And through it were the Stepping-stones of Truth. If only we could find them!"

"Never heard of them," said Trickery.

Dick Cowardly was in a terrible state. He clung on to Gracie, and she tried to shake him off. "You ought to be ashamed of yourself!" she scolded him. "Why, even the children behave more bravely than you. The worst of it is, you make us even more frightened when you show us you are so afraid yourself."

Suddenly a light showed not far off. It was the light from a lantern! Mr. Scornful hailed the light with joy.

"Hey there! We're lost in the marsh! Can you help us?"

A voice came over the marsh. "Are you from the Land of Far-Beyond? If you are, I will certainly help you."

There was a silence. Not one of the travellers was from the Land of Far-Beyond. All of them came from the City of Turmoil. Then Trickery answered, in a silky sort of voice.

"Friend, we *are* from the Land of Far-Beyond, and have lost our way. Help us!"

"We turned aside from the path to help some one who had lost the way!" cried Bluff, untruthfully. "And now we need help ourselves."

"We will pay you highly if you help us," called Harriet Gamble, who hadn't a penny in the world!

"How many of you are there?" cried the voice and the lantern flashed towards them. "Oh, quite a number. Well, three of you say you are from the Land of Far-Beyond, and I am allowed to help those. But what about the others? Are they also from my land?"

"We'd better say we are, or we shall be left here to drown," said Mr. Scornful, in a low voice to Dick and Gracie. But Peter answered first.

"I am not from the Land of Far-Beyond! But I want to go there, and have lost my way!" he cried, in a ringing voice. "Tell me where the path lies that goes through the marsh safely. I want to take my sisters to safety. They wish to go to the Far-Beyond Land too."

"I am allowed to help those who are on their way there," said the voice. "Go a little to your left, boy. You will come to some stones that are laid across the marsh to the path where I am."

Peter scrambled off to the left, his feet sinking in with a squelching sound as he went. With great joy he felt his foot scraping a big flat stone. He stood on it and held out his hand to Anna and Patience. He pulled them up beside him, and then caught the gleam of another white stone in the half-darkness. He jumped to it, and the girls came too. Then one by one the others clambered over the marsh to join them, and soon the whole company were safely on the Stepping-stones of Truth. Trickery, Bluff, and Harriet Gamble were the last, for they had sunk so deeply into the marsh that they found it difficult to make their way to the flat stones.

Peter led the way to where the lantern light shone steadily. By the time he reached it, night had fallen completely, and darkness lay all around. They had only just been rescued in time!

The boy was about to thank his rescuer when he heard yells from the marsh behind. The little company turned and strained their eyes through the darkness. The shouts came from Trickery, Bluff, and Harriet Gamble.

"Help! Help! We've lost the stones. We are sinking again!"

"You will soon find them!" cried the man with the lantern. "I am going to take these people safely from the marsh, and show them the rest of the stepping-stones. In any case, there is some one else coming along in a minute. He will help you!"

The man took up his lantern and led the way over rather damp ground to where more white stepping-stones lay. The children shivered, for the night was misty in the marsh. Peter was rather worried about the three left behind.

"Will they really find their way on to the stones again?" asked the boy.

"If they are honest folk, they will," said the man. "If they are not, it will do them no harm to spend a night amid the terrors of the Marsh of Dishonesty! I am Mr. Straight, and I always help decent folk – but Mr. Crooked will be along here soon too, and will help them out if necessary – but oh, what a dance he will lead them through the marsh, for he takes a great delight in deceiving others. And he will probably desert them in the middle of their trouble. It is very difficult to help people like your three friends there!"

"They are not our friends," said Anna. "We fell in with them, and they took us the wrong way. We wanted to get to the House of Peace by nightfall – but now we shan't, because it is dark already."

"No – you are right away from the House of Peace," said Mr. Straight, swinging his lantern so that its rays showed up the long line of white stepping-stones. "You will have to lie by the wayside to-night, and do your best to sleep there. My house lies on the other side of the marsh, or you could shelter there."

He brought them safely over the stepping-stones to hard ground. How marvellous it was to feel the earth solid and hard under their feet, instead of soft and treacherous!

"There is the narrow path again," said Mr. Straight, and he shone his lantern on to it. "There are high hedges just here, which keep off the wind. Rest there until daylight. I must go back into the marsh to see if there are any other folk to be helped. Good night."

He disappeared into the darkness, his lantern making a round speck of light that grew smaller and smaller as he walked over the marsh. Every one was very tired. It was much warmer now they had left the marsh, and the hedges made a sheltered spot. They all found as comfortable places as they could and sat or lay down to rest. Soon most of them were asleep.

"How easy it is to leave the path!" said Mr. Scornful to Gracie,

51

yawning widely. "Well – nothing will make me turn aside from it to-morrow. And I won't let any one else, either."

But he was wrong. All kinds of queer things happened to the little company the next day!

CHAPTER EIGHT

MR. INDUSTRIOUS AND THE WALL OF HARD WORK. THE DEMONS OF BOREDOM. LAZINESS AND SLOTH GET GRACIE GRUMBLE. RAGE, WRATH, AND TEMPER. THE STRANGE CASTLE

The sun shone down warmly when the five children awoke. At first they could not get up for they were so stiff with lying under the hedge. But after they had stretched themselves a little, they got up and ran about. There was still a little food left from the packages the Guide had given them and every one ate their share. They drank from a silvery stream that ran down from a hill.

"Now come along," said Mr. Scornful, trying to hoist his burden higher on his shoulders. "We should easily reach the House of Peace by the afternoon."

They all set out again. The path ran along between thick woods. No one ventured into them. The company kept well together, and sometimes sang songs to while away the journey.

Now, as they travelled, they heard the sound of voices in the distance, and they hurried along to see who was in front of them. To their great astonishment they found a number of people hard at work building a wall that ran along the right-hand side of the path.

"What are you building that wall for?" asked Mr. Scornful, in surprise.

"Well, the Village of Boredom lies just to the right of us," said one of the men, called Industrious. "And demons live there, who often come along to this path and waylay travellers. So all who pass by are now made to build a little on to the wall, to keep out the demons."

"Have we got to stop and do that too?" asked Gracie Grumble, impatiently. "We want to get on quickly!"

"This wall will help all travellers to get on more quickly," said Industrious. "You have no idea how the demons of Boredom hinder the traveller on his way to the City of Happiness."

"This must be the Wall of Hard-Work," said Mr. Scornful, looking at his map. "Very well. If we have to do our share, we'd better do it. Come along, children. You can help too."

Peter, Anna, and Patience set to work. Patience worked the best, and did not seem to mind how many bricks she carried for Mr. Scornful and Dick Cowardly. But Gracie Grumble, Lily, and John made a great fuss.

Gracie did her very best to upset every one by her grumbling and grousing. "If I knew I'd have to do this sort of thing I'd never have come," she grumbled.

"Hard work never hurt any one," said Industrious, building the wall a little higher. "Do your share, and help others on the way."

Some one came up to Gracie and whispered in her ear. "If you get tired, slip away with me. You can rest in my little house up the way."

Gracie turned and saw a sleepy-eyed woman looking at her. She was untidily dressed, and rather dirty. "I could do with a cup of tea," said Gracie.

"Well, you come along then, as soon as Industrious goes off to get his next lot of bricks," said the woman. "And bring any of your friends with you. I always say that Industrious works you poor travellers far too hard."

Lily and John had heard what was said. They pressed against Gracie. "Let us go with you," whispered Lily. "I'm tired of this. There are plenty of other people to do this work. No one will miss us!"

So, as soon as Industrious was out of the way, Gracie, John, and Lily followed the untidy woman to a little cottage tucked back from the path. They went up the front garden, which was full of weeds, and entered the house. A man was lying asleep on a sofa, his mouth wide open.

"Wake up, Laziness," said his wife, and gave him a poke with her fingers. "Here are some guests."

The man woke up and winked at the three guests. "So you've managed to escape your share of the work!" he said. "I don't blame you. Hurry up, Sloth, and make a cup of tea. I'm thirsty."

"Laziness and Sloth," whispered Lily to John. "I don't like the sound of these people."

"Oh, well, let's have a sit-down and something to eat and drink," said John, yawning. "I'm tired."

They sat down and sipped the cups of sweet tea that Sloth gave them. Then Lily stood up to go.

"What's the hurry?" asked Laziness, pushing her down again. "No hurry at all! Your friends outside won't go without you."

"But I ought to do my bit in building the wall," said Lily. "The demons of Boredom sound horrid, and I'd like to help in keeping them off the path we follow."

"Oh, don't worry about any demons," said Sloth. "They're not so bad. Why, good gracious me, we often have them in here, visiting us!"

"I don't think I'd like to meet any," said Lily, nervously. "I'm going. Come along, John, do. And Miss Grumble, you really must come with us!"

But Gracie was enjoying herself. She had been grumbling away to Sloth and Laziness, telling them of all the dangers and difficulties she had been through, and they had seemed really most interested.

"Don't you go," said Laziness, putting his hand on Gracie's arm. "Don't you go. You are a delightful person to have here. Isn't she, Sloth?"

She just suits our household nicely!" said Sloth, pouring Gracie another cup of tea. "Now you drink that, my dear, and rest your weary bones – and tell us all you want to."

Lily and John ran out of the cottage to join the others, and were soon hard at work. The wall was already a whole row of bricks higher. "This will keep out the demons nicely!" said Industrious. "They are such tiresome fellows, you know – they don't *hurt* the travellers, but they just make them feel dull and tired, and as if it really isn't worth while going on! It's a sort of spell they cast over passers-by. But this wall of Hard-Work will defeat them!"

After about four hours' work Industrious thanked Mr. Scornful, Dick, and the children, and bade them goodbye. "You can go on your way now," he said. "You have done your share!"

"Where's Gracie Grumble?" asked Mr. Scornful, looking round for her. "She seems to have disappeared. I missed her grumbling voice some time back!"

"She's in Sloth's cottage," said Lily. "We went too – but it was such a dirty, untidy place, and we didn't like Sloth, or her husband, Laziness. Shall we go and fetch her?"

"I will," said Mr. Scornful, and he went up to the cottage door and opened it.

Gracie was fast asleep in her chair! Mr. Scornful shook her hard. "Wake up! It's time to go! You haven't done your share of work, either – that's not fair of you."

"Oh, leave me alone," said Gracie, in her whining voice. "Always having to do something I don't want to do! I wish to goodness I could stay here for a while with these two new friends of mine."

"Well, you can!" said Sloth, at once. "We'd love to have you. We think you are good company. You stay awhile with us and have a good rest."

"Gracie, get up and come with us," said Mr. Scornful, impatiently. "Can't you see what sort of people these are? They're no good at all. I shouldn't think they've ever done a scrap of work in their lives, and they look as if they haven't any brains at all. Come along, now."

But Gracie could be very obstinate when she liked. "I'm not coming," she said. "I'm going to stay here for a few days. Then I'll come along by myself, or join up with other travellers."

"Well, we've got to get to the House of Peace before nightfall," said Mr. Scornful, "so I'm not going to waste any more time arguing with you. You're poor company at the best of times, making the way hard with your groans and moans and grumbles and whines. Maybe Laziness and Sloth will find that you suit them well!"

He stamped off up the path to Dick and the others. "She's not coming," he said. "Well, I'm not sorry!"

Nobody was, because Gracie really was a nuisance at all times. She made things harder by grumbling when difficulties came, and she spoilt the happy times by grousing and looking on the dark side.

"Well, we're only seven now," said Peter. "We have lost Mr. Fearful, Miss Simple – and now Miss Grumble. I'm afraid they'll never lose their burdens."

On they went again, the Wall of Hard-Work running along the way for miles. Sometimes they heard shouts on the other side, and guessed that they were the demons of Boredom trying to get across. But the wall kept them out.

As they went along, singing songs together, they heard loud shouts, and the sound of blows.

"Whatever's that?" said Dick Cowardly, in alarm. "Is it a fight?"

He got behind the others, for he was a timid fellow. Mr. Scornful pressed on, and when he came to a bend in the path he stopped. A fight was going on between three fierce-looking fellows – and what a fight!

The three men yelled and shouted as they struck at one another

A FIGHT WAS GOING ON BETWEEN THREE FIERCE-LOOKING
FELLOWS

56

with big sticks. Thwack, thwack! Bang, thud! Yells and groans came on the air, and the children stared in amazement at the fierce quarrel.

The men fell apart, tired out, and sat down, panting, glaring at one another with bloodshot eyes. Mr. Scornful went up to them.

"Whatever is the matter?" he asked. "Are you out of your minds, to strike at one another like that?"

"Temper flew out at me and hit me," said one man, sulkily, nursing a bruised hand.

"Rage called me evil names!" said Temper.

"Wrath kicked me," said Rage, and Wrath struck out at him with his stick at once. Then the fight started again and Mr. Scornful jumped back quickly, afraid of being hit.

The travellers had to wait till the fight was over, for the three men took up all the path with their battle. It was not a pleasant sight to watch. Rage was quite mad and really seemed to be trying to kill the others. Wrath was almost as bad, and Temper was spiteful, getting in sly blows here and there.

The fight came to a sudden end. All three gave each other such fearful blows that they fell to the ground, moaning.

"Water, water!" groaned Rage.

"My arm is broken!" wept Wrath.

"Help us, help us," begged Temper, his head bleeding from a blow from Rage's heavy stick.

"I don't see how we can help them," said Dick Cowardly. "We'd better go on."

"I don't like leaving them here like this," said Mr. Scornful, looking round to see if there was anywhere to take the groaning men.

"Take us to the castle over there, the one behind those trees," said Rage, trying to rise from the ground. "That is where we live. It isn't far. Help me along."

Mr. Scornful gave him his arm. The children then saw the strong walls of a castle rising above the trees on the left. Its towers overlooked the path they were on.

"We'll just help these men to their home and then go on again," said Mr. Scornful. "Dick, take that man's arm – and you two boys can help the third one. What a terrible quarrel they have had. It's a mercy they didn't all kill one another!"

The three men staggered from the path on to a broad drive that led between the trees to a great iron gate. Mr. Scornful swung the gate open and the little company passed through. They could then see the castle.

It was dark and forbidding-looking. The children didn't much like the look of it.

"I shouldn't like to go inside!" whispered Anna to Patience. But they had to! For when they reached the great door of the castle, it swung open and the three men invited the travellers inside.

"You have been so kind in helping us! Pray let us make you known to our master. He will give you a good meal and then set you on your way."

Mr. Scornful liked the sound of a good meal, so in he went, and the children had to follow. "Who is your master?" he asked the man – and they made a strange reply!

"Our master is – the great Giant Cruelty!"

CHAPTER NINE

CASTLE OF GIANT CRUELTY. THE GIANT AND HIS PAGE-BOY, FRIGHT. THE POOR PRISONERS. THE TRAVELLERS ARE FORCED TO STAY THE NIGHT. ANNA FINDS MERCY AND PITY. THE DUNGEONS. ESCAPE THROUGH THE TUNNEL OF DISGUST AND THE STEPS OF TEARS

Every one wanted to turn round and hurry away when they heard the name of the master of the big castle!

"Giant Cruelty! Mr. Doubt told us about him," said Anna, shivering, for she remembered the dreadful tales she had heard. "Oh, Mr. Scornful, please let's go back to the path. We've come away from it again! Horrid things always happen if we do that."

But it was too late, The great door swung shut, and when Mr. Scornful tried to open it, he could not. A loud voice called to them from a nearby room.

"Who is there? Is that you, Rage? Where have you been?"

"It is I, Master," answered Rage, hurrying to the room. "I and Wrath and Temper fell out with one another and some passers-by brought us here. I know you like to see visitors, so we have asked them in. They would be glad of a meal!"

"Come in!" cried the loud voice of the giant. Rage and Temper pushed the little company into the big room, whose ceiling was so high that it could hardly be seen. The fire in the room was smoking, and the smoke hung about the ceiling, and swirled around the big figure sitting on a kind of throne at the end of the room.

The giant was enormous, He had cruel, grasping fingers, and curiously small eyes that glinted spitefully as he looked down at the little company. He was dressed most magnificently. His lips were very thin and straight, and there was no kindness in him.

At his feet sat a small, miserable-looking page-boy, called Fright. Cruelty kept him busy all day long, and now, with a kick of his great foot, the giant sent him off to fetch something to eat and drink for the visitors.

Even Mr. Scornful was afraid of the giant Cruelty. "He is such a powerful fellow," he said to poor Dick Cowardly, who was trembling like a jelly beside him. "It is said that he can make thousands, nay millions of people, unhappy once he uses his power. We must be careful not to offend him."

Now when Fright brought back a tray of sandwiches, cakes and milk for the travellers, there came a curious noise from somewhere outside the room.

"Some one is crying and moaning," said Anna. The giant was rubbing his hands with pleasure.

"Ah, that is one of my prisoners," he said. "How I love to hear that sound! It is music in my ears."

"What! You love to hear some one in misery or pain?" cried Peter, thinking how easily the giant could capture them all and treat them wickedly.

"Who is that crying?" said Anna, uncomfortably. "I don't like it."

"I told you it was one of my captives," said the giant, his spiteful eyes glittering. "I think it is the prisoner Misery. Or it might be Poverty. They are always crying out, saying that I starve them."

A loud scream made every one jump. "Oh, that is Pain," said the giant, with a laugh. "I keep him captive too. He amuses me."

Peter felt cold all down his back to hear the giant say such cruel things. How awful to keep people prisoner and treat them so that they cried out like that! He gazed at the giant with such dislike that he noticed it.

"Ah, my boy, you don't like me when you meet me? But I have often been beside you in the City of Turmoil and you did not know it! I laughed when you threw stones at animals and

59

THE GIANT WAS ENORMOUS. . . . AT HIS FEET SAT A SMALL,
MISERABLE-LOOKING PAGE-BOY, CALLED FRIGHT

birds. I made merry when you struck some one smaller than yourself! I nearly cracked my sides when you stamped on frogs! And how I roared when you called unkind names after that poor blind woman who lived in the street next to you."

Peter went pale. He remembered all those things. He had done them. He had been cruel too – and the giant had been by his side, invisible, and had enjoyed all that he, Peter, had done. The boy was filled with horror. Tears came into his eyes, and he turned his head away. The other children gazed at him. They too remembered spiteful, cruel things they had done, unthinkingly, and they were filled with horror and disgust when they remembered them.

"How could we?" whispered Anna, quite unable to eat the cake she had taken. "How could we?"

"Come and see my captives," said Cruelty. "I'll make them dance for you."

"Oh, no, no!" cried Anna. "I don't want to see Misery and Poverty and Pain dancing for you! Leave the poor things alone. Set them free."

"Well, I've plenty of others for you to see if you like," said the giant, grinning suddenly, and showing a set of sharp, blackened teeth. "There's Famine and Starvation, and there's ——"

But the company had had enough of the giant. They rose up to go, Dick Cowardly trembling from head to foot.

"We must say good-bye," said Mr. Scornful, for once speaking in a low voice.

"Oh, no!" said Cruelty. "Oh, no! You must spend the night with me, I beg of you! Fright, take them to the spare-rooms, and see that they are comfortable."

It was not a bit of use trying to get away. The big door was fast shut. Rage, Temper, and Wrath stood beside it, looking very fierce. Fright led the travellers to two big rooms. One was for Mr. Scornful and Dick, the other for the five children. Every one was afraid.

"It's a pity that Cruelty is so very powerful," said Mr. Scornful to Dick. "He wields such a terrible power over every one. Hardly any one can withstand Cruelty."

There were beds for every one in the two rooms. Although it was not yet night the travellers thought it best to lie down and rest. But there was not much rest for any one in the giant's great castle! Cries and groans, sighs and moans filled the night, and at last Anna could stand it no longer.

She got up and went to the door. She looked out. All was dark save for the glimmer of a lantern set on a low wooden bench. She took it up.

"I'm going to set some of these poor people free!" thought the little girl, bravely. "I just can't bear to hear them crying out like this!"

She went down a long passage and came to a door that led into a quiet room. Here she found two women, dressed in long robes, whispering together. They started when they saw her, and then pressed their fingers on their mouths to sign to her to be quiet.

"Who are you?" asked Anna, in surprise, for the women had sweet faces and kind eyes, surprising to see in the giant's castle.

"I am Mercy and this is my twin-sister, Pity," said the first woman. "We come secretly at night to help the poor captives in this place. Cruelty knows nothing about us, so do not give us away. What is your name?"

"I am called Anna," said the little girl. The two women looked at one another and smiled.

"Do you know what your name means?" asked Mercy. "It means 'merciful, pitiful' – so you must be a small cousin of ours. Did you creep here to see if you could help the captives in the night?"

"Yes," said Anna. "I couldn't bear to hear their cries."

"Go and wake your companions," said Pity. "If you do not escape to-night, you will be made prisoners yourselves to-morrow. Bring your friends here to us."

Anna hurried quietly back to the bedrooms. She awoke the other four children, and Peter went to wake Mr. Scornful and Dick Cowardly. Silently they all made their way down the passage to the little room where Mercy and Pity awaited them.

"We shall have to take you by the dungeons where the captives are kept," whispered Pity. "But do not take their cries too much to heart, for we shall do our best to-night to help the prisoners, and maybe set one or two free."

Nobody liked going down a flight of long, dark, damp steps into the dungeons. Mercy and Pity both had glowing lanterns to light the way. Anna would not look at the captives, who cried out piteously as the little company went by!

"Oh, you *will* help them, won't you?" she asked Pity, taking the woman's hand. "You *will* help them!"

"We will," promised Pity. "We get money from many people in the world, and spend it on things to give to the poor prisoners. The more help we get from others, the more we are able to do."

"Oh, I will always give my money to help in future!" said Anna. "I shall know that you and Mercy are spending it well!"

Even Mr. Scornful was most uncomfortable as he heard the sighs and groans in the dungeons. He put his fingers in his ears as he hurried by. Dick Cowardly was in such a state of fear that he could hardly walk. He kept imagining that he too was in the dungeons, a prisoner of Giant Cruelty, and it made him quite terrified.

"How do we escape?" asked Peter, looking up into Mercy's sweet face. "We seem to be going down into the heart of the earth."

"There is only one way of escape from Cruelty," said Mercy. "I and Pity are the only ones who know it. It is through the Tunnel of Disgust, up the Steps of Tears, and out through the Gate of Kindness."

That was a queer journey! The travellers went down and down, and at last came to a queer tunnel, narrow and evil-smelling. Slime was under their feet and cold drops of water fell from the roof on to their heads.

"Oh, how I do hate this place!" cried Patience. "How I hate the Giant Cruelty! Oh, those poor prisoners of his."

"I detest it all so much that I feel sick," said Mr. Scornful. "I am disgusted, filled with loathing and contempt to think that any one should use their power to starve and torture other creatures."

Every one felt sick as they went through the Tunnel of Disgust. Every one was filled with loathing. How they longed to be outside the horrible castle!

The tunnel at last came to an end. A great flight of steps rose up from the door that led out of the tunnel. They were silvery and shining. "These are the Steps of Tears," said Mercy. "There are many to climb!"

"I'm glad to be out of that tunnel," said Anna. "I couldn't help hating and loathing that giant all the time I was walking in it. And now I feel so sorry for his captives that I want to cry!"

"I wish we could help them," said Lily, her eyes shining with tears.

"I mean to do all I can, when I hear of any one in trouble, in future," said Patience, going sturdily up the steps. "I've been mean and spiteful – yes, and cruel too – when I lived in the City of Turmoil – but now I am unhappy to think of people in misery."

Every one felt sad and made up their minds to do what they could to be kind if they had the chance at any future time. Mr.

Scornful blew his nose hard. He remembered many things that made him feel most uncomfortable. He remembered a little family he had ruined. He remembered a man whose job he had taken away. He remembered a beggar-woman he had laughed at.

They reached the top of the silvery steps at last. Mercy and Pity gazed round at the little company. What they saw in their faces pleased them. They led them to a small, well-oiled gate in the wall that surrounded the giant's grounds, and swung it open.

"Good-bye," said Mercy. "Remember us, and help us when you can!"

"We always will!" promised Anna. "And I won't forget what my name means. I am so pleased to know!"

"Good-bye," said Pity, and one by one the travellers passed out through the Gate of Kindness, and found themselves in the wood beside the giant's castle.

It was dark. The stars shone out in the sky, but no moon. Nobody knew the right way to go to get on to the path.

"We daren't stay here," said Mr. Scornful at last. "We may be taken prisoners again. Let us go deeper into the wood and sleep there. Then when daylight comes we can make our way safely back to the right path."

So into the wood they went, found a patch of soft ground where pine-needles made a bed for them, and lay down to go to sleep.

CHAPTER TEN

CAPTURE OF FRIGHT. MERRIMENT, GAIETY, AND LAUGHTER
ARE GOOD COMPANIONS. THE FORTUNATE RIDERS. ENVY,
JEALOUSY, AND SPITE JOIN THE COMPANY

But no one could sleep. Small noises kept them awake. Anna was sure she heard rustlings and whisperings near her. Dick was certain the giant's servants were looking for them to capture them. Peter kept glancing all round in the darkness, afraid for his sisters.

There came a noise so near Mr. Scornful that he jumped almost out of his skin! He made a grab at whatever it was so near him – and caught hold of some one small who squealed, wriggled, and kicked.

"Ah! Got you!" said Mr. Scornful. "What do you mean by

creeping around us like this, trying to scare us? Who are you?"

"I'm only the giant's little page-boy, Fright," said the little fellow, trying to wriggle out of Mr. Scornful's grasp. "Let me go!"

"Ho! So you are that nasty little creature, Fright, are you?" cried Mr. Scornful, and he shook the boy well. "Now, just listen to me, Fright. I shall tie you hand and foot with my rope until the morning, and then you can go back to your horrible master. Ho, now we've caught you, we can laugh at you! Coming round us at night to scare us like this! Wait till the morning, and how we shall smile at ourselves to think that a stupid little fellow like you could keep us awake all night!"

Once Fright was tied up, the little company felt happier. They settled down to sleep, and did not awake until the first birds began to sing. Then Peter sat up and rubbed his eyes. He yawned and remembered the adventures of the night before. He thought of Fright and looked around for him.

And as soon as he saw Fright in the broad daylight a curious thing happened to the page-boy. He melted away like sugar – and disappeared! It was the most extraordinary thing in the world. Peter stared and stared. Then he awoke Mr. Scornful.

"I say!" said Peter. "Fright's gone! As soon as I saw him in the daylight, he just melted away! There are only your ropes left. Where's he gone?"

"He's gone like bad dreams and night-worries go, I suppose," said Mr. Scornful in surprise. "It's a mistake to let Fright worry you at night – I've heard it said that he finds it difficult to face the daylight. All the same, we'd better get back to the path quickly, before the giant hears that we are gone, and sends Rage, Temper, and Wrath after us. Hurry up, every one."

It was not very difficult to find the right path, because the travellers heard voices that guided them. They came to the path and saw going along it three bright-faced people, dressed in gay tunics and hose. They danced along, singing, and one of them played a fiddle.

"I wish *we* could dance along as lightly as that," said Mr. Scornful. "But our burdens are so heavy that we can hardly even run! I wonder who these people are. They have no burdens on their backs."

The three merry people saw the travellers and hailed them. "Who are you?" they cried.

"I am Mr. Scornful," answered Scornful, and told the three the names of Dick and the children. "Who are you?"

"I am Merriment, and this is Gaiety, and he is Laughter,"

said Merriment. "We are very good company. Would you like to go with us? We are keeping to this narrow path."

"Oh, yes, do let us go with you," begged Anna, going up to Merriment, whose dancing eyes made her feel happy. "We had a terrible day yesterday, a sad, unhappy day. I feel as if I would like to listen to singing and playing now, and see you dance along."

So it was a very happy company that went along the narrow path that morning. Lily managed to dance a little, even though her load was heavy. Peter and the others sang in tune to the merry lilt of the fiddle, and the whole company laughed at the jokes of Merriment.

"We went to the Castle of Giant Cruelty yesterday," said Anna to Merriment. "Have you ever been there?"

"Never," said Merriment, his blue eyes clouding over. "Gaiety has never been there either, nor has Laughter. We could not possibly get inside, however much we tried."

"I do hope you keep with us all the way," said John, who loved the gay voice of Laughter, and his crinkly eyes.

"I hope so, too," said Laughter, and he tickled John a little and made him laugh. The whole company forgot their heavy burdens that morning and their feet almost danced along the way. It was marvellous to find such merry friends.

As they went along they heard the sound of horses galloping behind them. They turned in surprise and saw a rich company coming along. There were six people travelling on horseback, all richly dressed except for one, who was their servant. The horsemen galloped up to the travellers and called to them.

"Can you tell us how far we are from the Palace of Pleasure?"

The children stared at the horsemen, They had no idea at all where the Palace was, for they had never even heard of it.

Mr. Scornful did not know either, and neither did Dick Cowardly. But Merriment, Gaiety, and Laughter answered at once.

"Straight ahead, and the first turning to the right."

Two of the riders were children, a boy and a girl dressed in brightly coloured clothes. They were beautiful children, with laughing eyes. Peter and Anna looked at them enviously.

"How fine it must be to ride along this path instead of travelling along with heavy burdens on our backs," said Peter to Anna.

Mr. Scornful gazed at the riders too. Not so long ago he too had had horses of his own, and rich clothes. He had ridden whilst

HORACE KNOWLES....

"CAN YOU TELL US HOW FAR WE ARE FROM THE PALACE OF
PLEASURE?"

67

others walked. He remembered the old days, and longed to wear fine clothes and ride along laughing too.

"Sorry we can't offer you all a lift!" said the first horseman, a handsome man whose grand clothes became him well. His horse was a magnificent one, and reared up as he spoke. "Perhaps we shall meet you at the Palace of Pleasure?"

"We'll be there!" cried Merriment.

"We'll hurry and meet you!" shouted Gaiety.

"Look out for me!" called Laughter. The riders urged on their beautiful horses, waved a laughing good-bye, and galloped on down the narrow path. The travellers stared after them, and queer feelings began to stir in their hearts.

"I wish I was as pretty as that little girl," said Lily.

"Pretty! She wasn't pretty! She was an ugly little thing, really, but it was her beautiful clothes that made her seem attractive," said Anna, spitefully.

"Once I had as fine a horse as that man," said Mr. Scornful. "Now here I am walking along this silly path, with a tiresome burden on my shoulder! Some people have all the luck. Why couldn't *I* be that man!"

"I've never ridden a horse in my life," said Dick Cowardly. "And I should cut a sorry figure if I did. It doesn't seem fair that some people should do all these things and others never have a chance."

"I wish I had a horse to gallop on like that boy," said Peter, longingly.

"You wouldn't be able to ride it as well as he did," said John. "You'd fall off!"

"Of course I shouldn't" said Peter, indignantly. "I could gallop like the wind!"

Their three merry companions fell silent. Merriment's face grew solemn. Gaiety put away his fiddle. Laughter looked sad. The travellers talked for a long time about the gay riders, and then they suddenly saw that three more people had joined their company. They had come up so silently that no one had heard them.

They were not nice-looking companions! One was tall, thin, and sour-looking. The second was small, bent, and sullen. The third was a woman with a sharp face, greenish eyes, and a screwed-up mouth.

"Hallo!" said Peter, in surprise. "Who are you? I didn't hear you overtaking us."

"I am Envy, and this is my brother, Jealousy," said the tall,

68

thin man. "That is our companion, Sally Spite. We usually travel together."

"Are you going to the Land of Far-Beyond?" asked Anna, surprised.

"No. We are not really going anywhere," said Envy. "We just travel along with any one who will have us for company."

No one liked the three new travellers. As they journeyed along, Envy, Jealousy, and Spite said hurtful things about the others, and soon everyone was feeling bad-tempered and impatient.

"Let's ask Gaiety for a tune on his fiddle!" said Peter at last. "I feel all horrid inside somehow. I want a laugh for a change!"

But the three merry companions were gone! How queer! No one had seen them go. They had slipped away just as silently as the three new companions had come up. Every one stared around in astonishment, wondering where in the world Merriment, Gaiety, and Laughter had disappeared to.

"I didn't see them go," said Peter, disappointed not to see Merriment's bright, laughing eyes.

"They went down the turning that led to the Palace of Pleasure," said Envy. "I saw them go."

"We must have missed that turning," said Anna, in surprise. "Anyway, if it led away from the narrow path, we couldn't have gone down it. But I do wish Merriment and the others had kept on the way with us. They might at least have said good-bye."

"They will never walk with us," said Jealousy. "As soon as we appear, they always turn off and go away."

"They never agree with us," said Sally Spite, her green eyes gleaming like a cat's. "Never mind – we will go with you!"

"Oh, I don't know that we want you," said Peter, who didn't at all like Sally Spite's sharp tongue. "You'd better travel on by yourselves."

"Well!" said Envy, in a disagreeable tone. "Well! What bad manners you have! If you don't want our company, we will certainly leave you."

And with that Envy, Jealousy, and Spite walked rapidly on in front, and joined some other travellers, who were walking some way ahead. They disappeared down a path not far off, and Peter and the others wondered where they all went to.

They asked a man who was trimming the hedge, and he answered at once.

"Oh, that path leads to the House of Discontent. That's where Envy, Jealousy, and Sally Spite live, you know. They take travellers there, if they can. It's a good thing you got rid of them when you did, or you might have had to stay in their house for a while – and it's not a pleasant place, I can tell you!"

"We had a narrow escape!" said Peter. "Are we far from the House of Peace?"

"Not a great way," said the man. "Just keep straight on, and you'll come to it!"

CHAPTER ELEVEN

THE BAND OF SOLDIERS. THE THREE WARRIORS, QUARRELSOME, STRIFE, AND MALICE. DICK COWARDLY RUNS AWAY. GALLANT AND DARING FACE THE SOLDIERS

"We shall soon be at the House of Peace now," said Mr. Scornful, pleased. "We seem to have been looking for it for ages! It has such a nice name. I shall be glad to have a little peace, after our night in the giant's castle – and after hearing all the hurtful, spiteful things those last three companions of ours had to say!"

"I shall be gladder than any one to get to the House of Peace," said poor Dick Cowardly, who had not yet recovered from his stay in the castle, and was full of fears and frights.

"Oh, cheer up!" said Peter. "Things are never so bad as they seem!"

But Dick found it very difficult to cheer up. He walked on beside Mr. Scornful, bending beneath his burden, his eyes on the ground. Mr. Scornful had no patience with him.

"I've no use for any one with as little spirit as you!" he said to Dick. "Go and walk with the girls!"

So poor Dick shuffled behind to walk with the girls. They did not particularly want him with them either, but they put up with him, and tried to encourage him to look on the bright side of things.

"We'll soon be at the House of Peace," said Anna. "Stand up straight, Dick, and look up to the sky. See how blue it is to-day. Don't keep your eyes on the ground!"

"It can't be very far to the Land of Far-Beyond," said Lily, comfortingly. "Then you'll lose your burden and will feel happier."

Dick stood up straight and looked up to the blue sky. Then he dropped his eyes and looked ahead of him, trying to see if the House of Peace lay anywhere nearby.

He stopped. He gave a scream, and pointed to where something shone and glinted in the sun. "Soldiers!" he said. "Come to fight us and take us prisoner!"

Every one stopped. Sure enough, not far in front of them a band of soldiers barred the way. Their shields glittered in the sunlight, and their drawn swords shone brightly. Their helmets, set with plumes, shone too, and they stood immovable, waiting for the travellers to come up to them.

Mr. Scornful looked at the soldiers doubtfully. He wondered if they were a band belonging to the Giant Cruelty. He had no weapon to fight with, except his hazel staff, and that was of no use against swords.

"What are we going to do now?" asked Dick, his teeth chattering with terror.

"Look! There goes a man on horseback, trying to ride full-tilt at the soldiers!" said Peter, jumping out of the way as a fully armed rider galloped up behind him, his horse's hoofs tearing up the grassy path as he went.

Every one watched as the man clashed with one of the soldiers. Both had their swords drawn, and each hacked at the other. The man on horseback slashed viciously at the man on foot, and his horse kicked out at the others nearby.

But the soldier on foot fought back valiantly, and at last gave the horseman such a cut with his sword that the man gave a yell of pain. He turned his horse and rode off down the path again, his arm bleeding from a deep wound. He nearly rode down the astonished children.

No sooner had the man gone than two more came up on horseback, even more fully armed than the first man. Dick cried out in fear, for he was nearly trampled underfoot. Peter just had time to see the faces of the men. They were evil faces, with cruel eyes and tightly shut mouths. Then with a crash they were on the band of waiting soldiers, and galloped among them, trying to hew them down, and trample them under their horses' feet.

There was a great noise of battle, and the children watched open-mouthed as the foot-soldiers tried to surround the horsemen and defeat them.

"One man's off his horse!" cried Peter, in excitement. "There he goes – crash!"

The man fell to the ground, his sword clattering beside him. Six foot-soldiers at once jerked him to his feet and led him away. The other man fought on, but suddenly his sword splintered into two, and he gave up the fight. He set his horse to leap right over the soldiers around him, and it rose into the air on its powerful black legs.

The children scattered as the horse and rider thundered back towards them. The man hit out at them with his sword as he came by. Dick yelled with fear, for the tip of the sword went through his coat and slit it.

Then the horse of the other man came by, eager to follow its companion. It was riderless, for its owner had been taken prisoner. Dick caught hold of the bridle.

"I shall ride back on this horse," he said to the others. "I daren't stay here to face those soldiers. We shall be cut to pieces! We shall be taken prisoner! We shall be hauled off to the Giant's Castle."

"But you can't ride a horse! You said you couldn't!" cried Peter.

"Better to try and do that than face those fierce soldiers!" said Dick, trembling so much that he could hardly hold the horse. "Did you see how they slashed at the three riders? Did you see how they dragged off that man for their prisoner?"

"But, Dick, are you going to leave us?" cried Anna. She did not like poor Dick Cowardly, but it was not nice to see their little company getting smaller and smaller.

"I could get back to the City of Turmoil in a day on a horse," said Dick, trying to get into the saddle. "I'm used to my burden now. I want to go back home. I daren't face any more dangers. Better be safe in the City of Turmoil with this load on my shoulders than cut to pieces here by fierce soldiers!"

He got up on the horse's back, and took hold of the reins. The horse reared up, and Dick fell off backwards, landing with a bump on the ground. He yelled in pain.

The children ran to help him, but they could not help laughing. Dick was so silly and so helpless. They pushed him up into the saddle again, and told him to grip hard with his knees if the horse did any more tricks.

No sooner was he up in the saddle than the horse threw back its great head and neighed loudly. Then, with the terrified Dick clinging tightly to its back, it tore off at top speed down the path, away from the little company. They stood and stared after Dick and the horse, wondering where poor Dick would get to.

"It looks as if the horse meant to take Dick back to its own stable," said Mr. Scornful, watching the great animal as it suddenly turned to the left and galloped away from the narrow

THE MAN HIT OUT AT THEM WITH HIS SWORD AS HE CAME BY

path. "Dick can't guide a powerful creature like that. It will land him somewhere unexpected!"

"It certainly will," said a voice nearby, and Mr. Scornful turned to see two people standing near them. They were youths about twenty, bright-faced with wind-blown hair and dancing eyes. "That horse belongs to the knight called Strife, who is always galloping about upsetting every one. He has taken it into his head to try to get to the House of Peace to fight the owner, Content. I expect he'll escape from those soldiers, and will get back to his own house. He'll find your companion there, and lead him a dreadful life!"

"Poor Dick!" said Anna. "He will have a shock when he finds he is off the narrow path, going to a place he doesn't know – and if Strife goes back there, Dick will tremble like a jelly. Whatever will happen to him?"

"Oh, Strife will make him his servant," said one of the youths. He turned to his companion. "Come on," he said. "We must go on, and face these soldiers, Gallant."

"I'm ready, Daring!" cried the other youth, and took his companion's arm.

Mr. Scornful pulled them back. "You didn't see what happened to the horsemen who rode up to that band of men," he said. "Hadn't you better see if you can find a way round them, instead of walking right into them? That's what I've planned to do."

"There isn't a way round them," said Gallant. "Can't you see the thick hedge that bounds each side of the path just here? No one could get through that. Anyway, Daring and I always go straight for anything – we don't try to get round it. Come with us and try your luck.

But Mr. Scornful shook his head. He had no idea what he was going to do to get by the soldiers, who barred the narrow path – but he did know that he wasn't going to risk being killed by the flashing swords.

"You may have to go all the way back, if you don't go forward," said Daring, his bright eyes sparkling in the sunshine. "Come along with us!"

"I'll see what happens to you first," said Mr. Scornful pushing Daring's hand off his arm. So, shaking back their windswept hair, the two brothers advanced together, calling out a merry greeting to the soldiers.

"Hey, there! How goes the day with you? We are friends, and hope that you are too!"

74

"Aren't they bold and daring?" said Peter. The two youths walked right up to the soldiers, not in the least afraid of the drawn swords.

"Pass, friends, all's well," said the captain, and he sheathed his flashing sword, and clapped Daring on the back.

Gallant turned himself round and shouted back to the others, "Where do you want to go to?"

"Well, we want to find the House of Peace," shouted back Mr. Scornful. "But I'm sure those soldiers won't let us pass!"

Daring and Gallant doubled themselves up with laughter, and all the soldiers smiled broadly. The children looked in astonishment.

"What is the joke?" asked Peter at last.

"Well – these soldiers are *guarding* the House of Peace!" cried Gallant. "They belong to its owner, Content, and he employs them to keep away men like Strife and Quarrelsome, who disturb the rest of his household. You will be very welcome if you are friends!"

Mr. Scornful and the others felt suddenly very small and silly. So the soldiers were guarding the House of Peace! They were friends, not enemies. And to think the little company might have turned and gone back when they saw them!

"Poor Dick Cowardly," said Peter. "He could easily have stayed and gone with us. If only he had had a little more courage and had kept with us, instead of riding off on that horse belonging to Strife! I'm afraid we'll never see him again."

"Come along," said Mr. Scornful, striding forward, his head well up. "What Gallant and Daring can do, we can do too! These soldiers won't hurt us!"

CHAPTER TWELVE

THE HOUSE OF PEACE. CONTENT AND HIS WIFE, GLADNESS.
THREE GLORIOUS DAYS. THE TRAVELLERS SET OUT ONCE MORE
AND MEET TALKATIVE AND GOSSIP, BOASTFUL AND BRAG.
THE HOUSE OF NONSENSE

When the little company of six reached the soldiers, they were faced with drawn swords, but the faces of the men were friendly.

"Are you friends of our master, Sir Content?" asked the captain.

"We want to visit him and his House of Peace," said Mr. Scornful. "We are not enemies."

"Give me your word that you will not disturb the quiet of the House of Peace," said the captain. "It is the duty of us soldiers of Goodwill to guard our master's house from all that might disturb it. That is why we fight people like Strife, Quarrelsome, Envy, Jealousy, and Malice. We are always on the look-out for them – but peaceable folk may pass."

"We are peaceable folk," said Mr. Scornful. "We are on our way to the Land of Far-Beyond. We have not had very good fortune so far, and would dearly like a rest at the House of Peace."

"Pass, friends," said the captain, and he dropped his sword so that the point touched the ground. The other soldiers stood back, and a pathway was made for the six travellers to walk through.

Gallant and Daring were waiting for them. "What a mercy we weren't afraid, and walked boldly up to speak to the men!" cried Gallant. "It's no good being afraid of anything, however frightening it looks. Fortune favours the bold!"

"Well, I think you were very brave," said Peter, "How far is it to the House of Peace, Gallant?"

"Through this gate and over this meadow, and then across the little stone bridge to the house," said Daring, linking his arm in his brother's and in Peter's too. "Come along."

The eight of them set out together. They went through the white gate, and over a meadow studded with thousands of bright flowers. In the distance a stream gurgled, and beyond it rose a pleasant house, with cream-washed walls, thatched roof, and leaded windows.

"Doesn't it look restful?" said Anna, whose feet felt sore and tired.

"There are some cows!" said Lily. "We may have milk to drink."

"Look at those doves," said John, and he pointed to where a flock of white birds circled in the air around their tall dove-cote. Beside a pond set in a quiet courtyard six white pigeons strutted, their reflections shining perfectly in the water, on the top of which lay the waxen flowers of water-lilies.

"Oh, this is heavenly!" said Patience, stopping at the little stone bridge across the stream, to feast her eyes on the quiet house and garden. "If only we could stay here for a day or two. I feel as if my burden might become lighter!"

When they got to the house a tall, quiet-faced man, with deep brown eyes and a smiling mouth, came out to greet them.

BEYOND IT ROSE A PLEASANT HOUSE, WITH CREAM-WASHED
WALLS, THATCHED ROOF, AND LEADED WINDOWS

Behind him was his wife, Gladness, a sweet-faced woman with a lilting musical voice, and eyes that shone like stars.

"Welcome to you all!" said Content. His wife kissed the five children and exclaimed at their torn and dirty clothes.

"Poor lambs! You must stay here in our house for a while and let me wash your clothes for you! How tired you all look – except Gallant and Daring. I don't suppose they ever get tired!"

Every one went into the house. It was cool and quiet. The sun shone in at the windows, and lay in pools on the floor, and flowers were everywhere in tall vases and shallow bowls. It was a most beautiful house.

Upstairs were cool bedrooms, with soft-coloured curtains and inviting beds. Here again there were flowers, and the children loved the pictures on the walls and the soft carpets on the floors.

"What a rest it will be for us to stay here!" said Peter. "I feel dirty and tired. I would like a good bath – but I don't see how I can have it, with this burden on my back."

However, in some deft way of her own, Gladness managed to give all the tired children a warm bath, and to dress them in simple tunics whilst she had their dirty clothes washed and mended. She brushed their tangled hair, and gave them a meal of creamy milk, new brown bread, home-made jam, golden butter, and fresh fruit. Even Mr. Scornful did not turn up his nose at the simple fare, and ate as much as the others.

Gallant and Daring spent one night at the House of Peace, and then went on their way, singing in their musical voices. The company were sorry to see them go, for they had hoped to have them as companions.

"Oh, they won't wait for any one," said Sir Content. "They must always be up and doing! Now you must stay for three days, and then you will be rested. There are many more difficulties and dangers on the way to the City of Happiness, and you must be strong enough to meet them."

So for three glorious days the children and Mr. Scornful stayed with Content and Gladness in the House of Peace. It was a wonderful holiday. It was lovely to wake with the sound of the doves cooing outside, and to look out of the window and see the fat cows grazing peacefully in the meadows.

"I shall never want to live in a town again," said Anna. "There is always noise and dirt and discontent there. Here, in this peaceful countryside, there is beauty and quiet and gladness."

"Ah, you will find discontent and wickedness even in the countryside," said Sir Content, who was beside her. "It is ourselves who can keep the peace – or spoil it. What is the use of having beauty and peace around us if we have none in our own hearts? It is possible to live anywhere and have peace and happiness."

Every one was sad when the time came to go. Gladness dressed them in their own clothes again, cleaned and mended. She slipped them cleverly over their burdens, and sighed as she felt how big the loads were.

"Poor children! You will be glad to get rid of these terrible burdens."

"They haven't felt so heavy on our shoulders whilst we have been in the House of Peace," said Anna.

"No burdens feel so heavy here," said Gladness as she kissed the children good-bye. "Now, go on your way and keep to the right path. Come and see us again if ever you want a holiday. Content and I can always be found in our House of Peace."

They all felt sad to leave the restful house with its cooing doves, quiet pond, and pleasant garden. They set off down a little green path that led back very quickly to the way they had to follow.

Soon they were on the narrow path again, and trudged along with their burdens. There were but six of them now, and Mr. Scornful was the only grown-up left.

"I hope no more of us get left behind," said Peter. "We seem such a small company now. We must stick together."

"I didn't think I'd be left to look after a pack of children!" said Mr. Scornful. "You'd better all do as you're told, or I'll not walk with you!"

Mr. Scornful was feeling the weight of his burden again. He had not noticed it so much whilst he had been in the House of Peace, but now it weighed very heavy indeed, and he felt bored and bad-tempered.

The children fell behind. They did not want to walk with him if he felt like that. They talked quietly among themselves. Mr. Scornful felt more and more bored with his own company. So when he saw a man and a woman in the distance, he hurried to catch them up, and bade them good day very politely.

"My name is Scornful," he told them. "I am on the way to the City of Happiness. Who are you, and where do you travel to?"

"My name is Talkative, and this is my wife, Gossip," said the man, taking off his hat politely. "We are meeting two friends of ours in a little while, Boastful and Brag. Do walk with us, for you must be bored to travel only with children."

Mr. Scornful was delighted to have company. The man was a wonderful talker, and the woman had all kinds of interesting news to tell him. She had often been to stay in the City of Turmoil, and she knew a great many of Mr. Scornful's friends there.

"Yes, I knew Mr. Success," she said, "and Mrs. Climb-High was quite a friend of mine. But after I found out that she didn't pay her bills, I wasn't friends with her any more."

"Oh, didn't she pay her bills?" asked Mr. Scornful, quite interested. "Well, well – to think of that! And she always boasted of her wealth, too! Did you know Miss Snob?"

"Oh, yes," said Gossip. "She always looked down her nose at any one who hadn't a cousin or somebody with a title. And how tired I used to get of hearing her say she had danced with the prince! If she knew how people laughed at her!"

Mr. Scornful had always thought Miss Snob a wonderful person. Now he felt quite pleased to meet somebody who pulled her to pieces. He went on talking eagerly to Gossip and Talkative, thoroughly enjoying himself.

Soon the three of them caught up with two men, who were introduced as Boastful and Brag. The five walked on amiably together, and the children behind heard the sound of their voices as they walked along together.

"Yes," they heard Boastful say. "Yes, I once had a house with a hundred bedrooms, and I kept two hundred servants. There was always a horse for every guest to ride, and a servant for every guest too."

"You should see the clothes we wore," went on Brag, who was as good as his brother at telling marvellous stories. "I had a cloak lined with pure gold."

"Wasn't it heavy?" asked Mr. Scornful in amazement.

"Very," said Brag. "I had to get four servants to hold it up for me when I walked. We always had gold plates and dishes on our dinner-table too. What a pity you can't come and stay a while with us, so that we might show you all our possessions."

Mr. Scornful did not want to be out-done in this talk of grand things, He too had been wealthy, and so he began to talk loudly of his twenty gardeners, his beautiful black horse, and his magnificent dinner-table, which would seat two hundred people.

But the others did not want to hear, and they interrupted him continually, so that he became cross. Meanwhile the children were calling out behind him, which made him crosser still.

"Are you nursemaid to these brats?" asked Brag, with a grin.

"They are nothing to do with me," answered Mr. Scornful angrily. "We all started out in a company together, and one by one the other grown-ups fell out, until only I and the five children were left. Let them shout! Let them call!"

The children were most distressed. Mr. Scornful had been so busy talking and boasting, and listening to the others, that he had not noticed the path he was taking. Now all of them had left the narrow path, and were travelling in the wrong direction. The children had noticed it very soon, and were shouting to Mr. Scornful to stop and turn back.

"Mr. Scornful! Mr. Scornful! We're on the wrong path! Please stop and turn back! *Mr. Scornful!*"

"I'll turn back and whip you all!" cried Mr. Scornful, in a rage. "Be quiet! I don't want to listen to you!"

The children stopped and wondered what to do. Did Mr. Scornful know they had left the path? Were his new friends showing him a short cut? What was happening?

In the end Peter ran after him and caught hold of his arm. "Mr. Scornful! Please listen! We're on the wrong path!"

Mr. Scornful heard then what Peter said. He stopped and looked around. He could not see the right path anywhere!

"How tiresome!" he said. "I was so interested in listening and talking – yes, and in boasting too – that I didn't notice where I was going. Hey, Brag – we've come the wrong way. Do you know the right way back to the path?"

"We're not keeping to that path," said Bragg with a grin. "We can't be bothered to for long. We're going on home. We live just here – look, there's our house. Come along in and have something to eat."

"Well, I suppose we may as well," said Mr. Scornful, and the five children went with him to Brag's house. It was a very noisy house, full of people who all talked at the top of their voices. They were all dressed grandly, but the children, with their sharp eyes, noticed rags peeping from under many a grand frock. The cuffs of some of the men's shirts were frayed too, and their shoes were cracked.

"They're not so grand as they make themselves out to be!" whispered Anna to Peter. "And aren't these sandwiches horrible! The bread is as stale as can be."

Mr. Scornful soon got tired of all the noise. He got up to go. Gossip and Talkative got up too. They had come in with the others.

"I'm sorry you are leaving my House of Nonsense so soon,"

said Brag, politely, as he and Boastful said goodbye. "We always think it is such an entertaining place. Plenty of people like to come here!"

"Thank you, but we must go on," said Mr. Scornful, feeling suddenly tired of all the silly talk he had heard. "Good-bye!"

"Our house is just down the way," said Gossip, taking Scornful's arm. "Just come in and have a sit-down there. We can give you better sandwiches than you will ever get at that tiresome Brag's."

"Dear me, I thought you were such good friends of Boastful and Brag," said Mr. Scornful, in surprise. "Now you talk against them!"

"Come along," said Talkative. "We'll set you on the right way to the path after you've visited our cottage."

CHAPTER THIRTEEN

CHATTER COTTAGE. FLATTER LEADS THE COMPANY TO THE
MEADOWS OF CONCEIT. COMMON-SENSE AND HIS PLANKS OF
HUMILITY

There was nothing to do but to go with the two of them. Soon they reached a pleasant little red cottage, with a name on the gate.

"Chatter Cottage," read Anna. "What a funny name! But don't you think it suits Talkative and Gossip, Peter?"

Outside ran a little stream. "That's the brook Babble," said Talkative. "It runs outside our cottage day and night, and we love to hear the noise it makes."

The children soon got bored inside the cottage. Gossip and Talkative gave them biscuits that were far too sweet, and some lemonade that was so thick and syrupy it was difficult to drink.

"Those biscuits and that lemonade were made by our daughter, Flatter," said Talkative. "Look – there she is. She will walk a little way back with you. She is such a sweet creature."

At first sight every one liked Flatter very much. She was pretty, with wide-open eyes, a smiling mouth, and a very nice way of listening to every one, as if they were saying really clever things.

"So you are all on your way to the Land of Far-Beyond!" she said, when she was introduced. "How brave of you to travel so far! I think you are marvellous!"

Every one felt pleased. Anna showed her her burden.

"Poor darling!" said Flatter, feeling it. "To think that a pretty little lamb like you should have to carry such a weight!"

Peter told her how they had escaped from the giant's castle, and Flatter's eyes nearly fell out of her head as she listened.

"Oooh, what a dreadful tale!" she said, when Peter had finished. "Oh, I do think you are all brave! Oh, how frightened it makes me feel to think of that dreadful Giant Cruelty! How wonderful you all are! How too, too marvellous!"

They set out with Flatter to go back to the right path. She had made them all drink some more of her terribly syrupy lemonade before they started, and soon Anna and Lily felt sick.

They lagged behind, feeling ill, but the others went eagerly on with Flatter, drinking in all the nice things she said to them in her sugary voice.

"How marvellous! How wonderful!" they heard her say, again and again, as they struggled after the others, feeling ill. Mr. Scornful had thrown out his chest, and was feeling grand. It was fine to be told he was marvellous. Peter, John, and Patience liked it too, and they listened eagerly for Flatter to tell them sweet things as well.

Suddenly Anna and Lily, who were still behind, heard Peter cry out, "Look out! These meadows are under water!"

The little company in front stopped. Flatter took hold of Mr. Scornful's arm and turned her pretty, wide-open eyes on him.

"Oh, dear! I've been so pleased at talking to you dear things that I've led you into the Meadows of Conceit. I forgot that they are flooded just here! Dear Mr. Scornful, could you please carry me over them? I don't want to get my feet wet."

Mr. Scornful didn't at all want to carry anything more than his burden, and he felt very vexed with Flatter at bringing them into flooded meadows. He picked her up in his arms. She looked such a dainty, pretty little thing – but once he had to carry her over the Meadows of Conceit she felt very heavy indeed!

He waded out into the meadows. Peter, Patience, and John followed, their feet splashing in the shallow water.

Lily and Anna did not follow. "Let's wait and see the way they get out and then follow," said Anna. "How stupid of Flatter to lead us wrong. She talks too much!"

The others waded into the meadows, but no matter in what direction they went they could not seem to come to drier ground.

AT FIRST SIGHT EVERY ONE LIKED FLATTER VERY MUCH. SHE WAS
PRETTY, WITH WIDE-OPEN EYES. . . .

Mr. Scornful turned round and saw Lily and Anna standing far behind.

"Go and get help!" he shouted. "We can't splash about here all day."

Anna and Lily looked around to see if there was any one to help them. A man was working in a field not far off. They ran to him.

"Oh, please," they said, "could you come and help? Some friends of ours are splashing about in the water-meadows there and can't get out."

The man, whose name was Common-Sense, looked up. He took up his stick and went with Anna and Lily to the edge of the flooded meadows. He set his hands to his mouth and shouted to the others.

"I'll get some planks for you and lay them across the meadow. I know the least-flooded bits."

He went to a pile of curious planks lying neatly stacked behind a hedge. They were very thin and shiny, and the two girls did not think they would take the others safely out of the meadows.

"They don't look as if they are made of wood," said Anna.

"They are not," said Common-Sense. "They are made of a rare stuff called Humility. Humility can always get people out of the flooded Meadows of Conceit."

Common-Sense flung down plank after plank, running lightly along them himself, until he had made a thin and narrow way to where the others splashed in the cold water.

"Come along!" he said. "Walk carefully, and you will reach dry ground."

Mr. Scornful stepped on a plank first, but as he could not see where he was going, because he was still carrying Flatter, he promptly slipped right off the curious plank and fell heavily into the water.

Then Flatter showed her other side and began to call Mr. Scornful all kinds of horrible names. He was shocked and surprised.

"Don't take any notice of her," said Common-Sense. "Leave her in the water. Her first name is Flatter – but her second name is Deceit! She is always leading people into these flooded meadows, and I am always having to rescue them."

"Well, thank you, Common-Sense, for coming to our rescue," said Peter, trying to keep his feet on the planks as he walked along. "How difficult it is to walk along these strange planks! I do feel ashamed now to think that I listened to all the silly nonsense that Flatter talked. She made me feel that I was the most wonderful boy in the world!"

Along the thin and narrow planks of Humility walked the three children and poor Mr. Scornful, who was very wet, very cold, and very ashamed of himself. Once Patience slipped off into the water, when she remembered some of the flattering things she had listened to – but she was soon back on the plank again, determined to get out of the treacherous Meadows of Conceit.

"Let me take you back to your path," said Common-Sense, who had followed behind the company, picking up his thin, narrow planks as he went. He seemed to be able to carry dozens on his shoulder without difficulty.

"We'd be very grateful if you would," said Mr. Scornful, stepping off the last plank thankfully. Every one but Anna and Lily took off their wet shoes and stockings and slung them round their necks to dry. Peter looked back to where Flatter was standing weeping in the flooded meadows, calling for help.

"Don't take any notice of her," said Common-Sense. "She loves these meadows, and can get out of them whenever she wants to. She knows them by heart!"

It was painful to walk back to the right path without shoes and stockings. It was very hard, and there were groups of horrid prickly little plants that the four without shoes kept treading on.

"Those are the prickly little plants called Shame," said Common-Sense. "They are not pleasant to walk on. Never mind – you are nearly at the right path. Then you will be quite all right!"

And in about half an hour they were on the narrow path, once more, feeling very grateful for the stout help of Common-Sense!

CHAPTER FOURTEEN

THE THUNDERSTORM OVER THE PLAINS OF WEARINESS. THE
COMING OF DISMAY AND DESPAIR. PATIENCE WALKS ALONE.
THE CASTLE OF DESOLATION AND THE CELLARS OF GLOOM.
PATIENCE FINDS CHEERFUL, COMFORT, AND COURAGE. THEY
GO TO RESCUE THE PRISONERS

"Now," said Mr. Scornful, when the six of them had said good-bye to Common-Sense, and were once again walking safely on the narrow path. "Now! We don't leave this path again at all! Not for anything or any one."

"Well, Mr. Scornful, we didn't want to leave this morning, but you went on and on with Talkative and Brag and the others, without hearing us shout to you," said Peter. "We'll really be careful now. We ought to be getting near the Land of Far-Beyond soon, if only we keep safely on our way."

That made every one feel cheerful. Anna and Patience began to sing. Mr. Scornful and the boys whistled in tune. Every one felt good-natured, ready to help the others along.

"My shoes and socks are dry already," said Peter, and he sat down to put them on. The others put theirs on too. The sun had soon dried the wet things.

But the sun, alas, deserted the travellers soon after that. A big black cloud blew up from the west, and another, and then another. Soon the whole sky was overcast, and the clouds hung lower and lower.

"There's going to be a storm," said Anna, half-afraid "Oh, dear – how unfortunate we are! We always seem to be running into something unpleasant!"

The storm soon burst. There was a roll of thunder from the sky, and a flash of vivid lightning. Then great drops of rain fell, and stung the travellers on their faces.

"Of course, we *would* be walking through a stretch of country where there isn't a tree or a hedge!" said Mr. Scornful, in an exasperated voice. "There's absolutely nowhere to shelter at all. We shall get soaked."

The path ran through a desolate stretch just there, with rough tussocks of grass sticking up, and great rocks lying around. There was no bush, no hedge, no tree. The path ran winding around the big rocks, easy to see because it was narrow and well-trodden.

The rain poured down now. The drops were so big that Patience gasped as they struck her cheeks. She shook her wet hair and plodded on.

The lightning flashed vividly, and the girls were all frightened. So were the boys, although they did not show it. Mr. Scornful was not afraid of a storm, but he was angry and dismayed at the soaking he was getting.

They all plodded on. There was nothing else to do. They could not just sit down on the wet ground and wait for the storm to blow over. Anyway, it showed no signs of going at all.

"This is dreadful!" said Anna, in despair, as she squeezed out her frock. "I am soaked through."

"And look at me!" said Peter, in great dismay. "There isn't a thread on me that isn't dripping wet. And now the wind is blowing terribly cold – we shall all get dreadful chills!"

Mr. Scornful sneezed so loudly that every one jumped in alarm. "I shall get one of my chills and be in bed for weeks," lamented Mr. Scornful. "Then you'll all have to go on without me."

The children felt dismayed to hear this. They were not fond of Mr. Scornful, but they had got used to him and he was the only grown-up left to guide them on their way.

Just then they heard the patter of footsteps behind them, and up came two people carrying huge umbrellas. Peter looked at them enviously.

They were not very pleasant people to look at. Their faces were full of fear, and they kept looking all round them as if expecting something dreadful to happen.

"Good day," said the first man, whose name was Dismay. "Have you got caught in this fearful storm? I and Despair always get caught in it when we cross the Plain of Weariness."

"Yes, it's a funny thing – but the sun always goes in over this plain," said Despair, his sad-looking eyes gazing mournfully at the travellers. "It's such a miserable stretch of country – it could do with plenty of sun and warmth – but no, in goes the sun, up come the clouds, down comes the rain – and in no time at all travellers are soaked to the skin!"

"Let us come under your umbrella," said Anna, shivering, and she and Lily crept under the big umbrella that Despair held over his grey head. Mr. Scornful and the two boys went under Dismay's big umbrella – but Patience walked on in the rain, looking up every now and again to see if the sun was peeping behind a cloud.

"I'm so wet already that I can't get any wetter!" she called.

It wasn't very pleasant under the big black umbrellas of Despair and Dismay. To begin with, it was very very dark under them, and although they certainly kept the rain off, it was difficult to see where they were going. Despair and Dismay kept their umbrellas well down in front, and the travellers could only hope that the two knew their way well enough to keep to the narrow path.

"I think the rain has stopped," said Mr. Scornful at last, and he stepped out from under the big dark umbrella. It *had* stopped – but what was this! They were no longer on the narrow path, but had once again wandered right away from it, hidden under the wide-spreading umbrellas of Despair and Dismay!

"We're off the path again!" cried Peter, in alarm. "Oh, it's too bad! We'll never, never get to the Land of Far-Beyond at this rate!"

"You never will," said Despair, in his miserable voice "Hardly any one ever does. It's danger, danger all the way – and at the end, what's to be found? Nothing much, I can assure you!"

"We're going to get back to our path," said Mr. Scornful, in a very resolute voice. "I don't know how I've been so silly as to allow myself to get off it again. Which is the way back, my man?"

"I don't know," answered Despair, shading his eyes and looking all round. "But look – there's a castle not far off. Let's go to it and ask our way."

"I'm not very fond of castles," said Mr. Scornful, doubtfully. "Whose castle is that?"

"I don't know," said Dismay. "We'd better go and find out. Anyway, you must get your clothes dried in front of a fire, or you'll all get chills, and then you won't be able to travel for weeks."

Mr. Scornful sneezed loudly again. His throat felt sore. He began to be alarmed about himself. Suppose he fell ill on this journey? Who would look after him? This would never do.

"We'll go to the castle and find out where we are," he said. And then, to every one's surprise, he suddenly said, "Now where in the world is Patience?"

No one had missed her up to that moment. They had been so busy walking under the big umbrellas, and looking at the big castle not far off that they hadn't noticed that Patience was not with them.

89

"Goodness! She must have gone on by herself in the rain without us," said Peter in alarm. "We'd better go after her."

"But we don't know where she has gone," said Anna, her eyes filling with tears. Every one stared round in great dismay. It was dreadful to lose Patience suddenly like this.

"Come on," said Despair, taking Mr. Scornful's arm in a firm grip. "Let's get into the castle before the next rainstorm. There's one coming. We can't be worse off than we are now. Maybe your little friend will turn up soon."

So they all went to the castle gates. The two enormous iron gates opened silently in front of them as they came near. It was rather strange. They all went in and the gates shut silently behind them. They went up a steep flight of steps to a great wooden door, studded with enormous blunt-headed nails.

That, too, opened silently. Mr. Scornful and the children hung back, half-afraid – but Despair and Dismay, suddenly strong, pushed them all inside, and the door shut behind them.

And then their two mournful companions took every one by the arm, and hurried them down a long dark passage into miserable cellars! Down slimy steps they were pushed, and on to cold stone floors from which frogs hopped away by the dozen!

"Where are you putting us?" cried Mr. Scornful, trying to force his way up the slimy steps. But Despair pushed him back, and laughed a horrid laugh.

"This is the Castle of Desolation, and we have put you into the Cellars of Gloom! Stay here for a year or two and let us hear your moans and sighs! Dismay and I love to hear those. They are sweet sounds in our ears!"

Then there came the sound of a key being turned in the lock, and the five travellers were prisoners in the horrid Castle of Desolation. Then indeed they felt lonely and desolate, sad and gloomy. How were they to escape? Where was Patience and would they ever see her again? How they hated Dismay and Despair, the two treacherous companions who had taken them so easily from the path!

"If only little Patience doesn't get taken prisoner too, by those horrid men," sobbed Anna. "I do wonder where she is. She wouldn't come under our umbrellas, so I didn't see where she went."

Patience was a long way away. She had plodded on in the rain, shaking the wet from her hair when it hung there in drops, trying to be cheerful. She had not at all liked the looks of Dismay and

Despair, and didn't want to go near them, even for the sake of sharing their big umbrellas.

"No," she had thought, "I'd rather plod on by myself! I can't get any wetter. I might as well be wearing a bathing-suit, I'm so wet!"

After a while Patience missed the sound of the feet and voices of the others, and she turned round to see where they were. And they were not there! She stood and stared in the utmost amazement.

"Well, where can they have gone?" she wondered. "They said they weren't going to leave the path – but they must have. And they didn't tell me! Oh, dear – what am I to do?"

She went back a little way, and then saw that footprints led off the path to the left. The little girl stood there, wondering whether or not to follow them.

"Nothing good ever happens when we leave the path," thought Patience. "But I can't go on alone! Maybe I'll come to some house or other and can ask for help."

So the little girl went plodding on down the path by herself, trying to keep cheerful and not to worry too much. She came to a stream that ran right across the path and splashed through it, hoping it would not get too deep. She came to a very rocky part, and had to climb patiently over masses of big rocks that seemed to have fallen from the hill nearby. It was hard and tiring work, but Patience set her teeth and determined not to give up.

Soon she heard some one calling to her. She turned and saw a merry-faced woman. "Hallo!" cried the woman, scrambling over the rocks to Patience. "Do you want any help? Who are you, all alone in this part of the country!"

"My name is Patience," said the little girl, and she told the merry-faced woman how she had lost her companions. "Who are you? Will you help me?"

"I am called Cheerful," said the woman, and she took Patience's hand. Things seemed much brighter suddenly. The rain stopped. The sun came out. Patience felt warmer, and she liked the feel of the woman's firm hand.

"Come to my cottage for a few minutes and dry your clothes," said Cheerful. "My sister Comfort lives there, and she will help you."

Patience trusted Cheerful and went willingly with her to a pretty little cottage set by the path. Indoors was another sweet-faced woman, the sister of Cheerful. Comfort took off the little girl's wet clothes and dressed her in a big old dressing-gown, warm and cosy. She gave her hot milk to drink and ginger biscuits to nibble. She listened whilst Patience told her how she had lost the others.

When the little girl described the two sad-faced, mournful men who had come up with their big umbrellas, Comfort gave a cry.

"Why, those were Dismay and Despair. They roam around the Plains of Weariness, and take as many travellers as they can to their castle of Desolation. They put them into the Cellars of Gloom. Only people who are determined enough, or patient enough, can get safely through the Plain without being taken off by those two horrid old men!"

"Well, my name is Patience, so maybe that is why I got through safely," said the little girl.

"Of course!" said Comfort, kissing her. "You must have been a good patient little thing to come along all this way by yourself."

"How can I help my brother and sister, and the others?" asked Patience, drinking her hot milk. "I can't leave them locked up in the Castle of Desolation. Can't we rescue them?"

"Yes," said Cheerful. "Our cousin Courage will soon be here on his evening visit. He has managed to get hold of the keys of the castle doors, and often rescues the poor prisoners there if he hears of them. After you are dry and warm, we will go with you, and Courage shall take us to the castle."

"Will Despair and Dismay fight us?" asked Patience, half-afraid. But Cheerful shook her bright head.

"They always run for miles when they see Courage coming – indeed they would run away even if they saw *you*, Patience – and they can't bear either me or Comfort. Eat up your biscuits. Our cousin Courage will soon be here."

Not long afterwards there came the sound of a cheerful whistling and into the little cottage came a stout, smiling youth, his eyes looking very straight at Patience. He was big and strong, and his mouth was determined.

His cousins told him about Patience and her lost companions. "We are sure that they must now be locked up in the Cellars of Gloom," said Comfort. Courage laughed and took some enormous keys from his pocket. He jangled them together and held them out to Patience.

"My keys will open any cellar in the Castle of Desolation!" he said, in his determined voice. "Shall we go now? You must come with me, for you may be of help."

The four set out and after a while came to where the trail of footsteps left the path. The rain had begun again and the four

HE WAS BIG AND STRONG

found it difficult to walk over the rough grass towards the big castle that loomed up out of the mist across the plain.

They came to the enormous iron gates. Courage fitted one of his keys into the lock. He turned it – and the gates swung open. They went through and up the steep flight of steps. Another of Courage's keys fitted the lock of the nail-studded door, and that opened easily too.

Inside the dark hall were Dismay and Despair, amazed at their unexpected visitors.

"Run at them, Patience! Laugh at them, Cheerful, and Comfort!" cried Courage. "I will be ready to strike them down if they show fight! But they are cowards at heart."

He was right. Despair and Dismay gave a scream of alarm, and fled away into the heart of their dark castle. Courage laughed a ringing laugh that echoed cheerfully down the long hall.

"They can never face me!" he said. "Now we will visit the cellars. I am sure your poor friends are there!"

His last key fitted the lock on the cellar doors – and down at the bottom of the steps were the five travellers, amazed to see the four at the top!

"Patience!" cried Peter, joyfully. "You've found us."

"I've brought Courage along with his great keys to unlock the doors and the gates," said Patience, hugging Anna and Peter as they came scrambling up the steps. "Hurry out, now – I've found a lovely cottage where you can dry your clothes and rest awhile. It belongs to Comfort and her sister Cheerful."

So, in great delight, the five rescued travellers followed Courage back to the cottage, shivering with cold and wet, but warm at heart to think of brave little Patience, and all the trouble she had gone to, to save them from the Castle of Desolation, and their two horrible captors, Dismay and Despair.

CHAPTER FIFTEEN

A PLEASANT NIGHT. HASTY AND HURRY COME TO GRIEF.
CAUTIOUS, PRUDENT, AND CAREFUL. A GAY CITY. A WONDERFUL
PROCESSION. LADY EXTRAVAGANCE AND LORD ARROGANCE.
LILY AND JOHN LEAVE THE COMPANY. A GREAT DISAPPOINTMENT

Comfort and Cheerful were pleased to put up the five children
and Mr. Scornful for the night in their pleasant little cottage.

"It will be a bit of a squeeze, but never mind!" said Comfort,
who made a joke of everything, and didn't seem to mind turning
her kitchen into a bedroom for five children. "Mr. Scornful can
go to our cousin Courage for the night – but I and Cheerful will
look after you five, and see that you set off tomorrow dry and
well-fed."

"We meet very nice people on our way as well as very nasty
ones," said Patience, giving Comfort a hug. "And the nice ones
more than make up for the nasty ones!"

Every one was glad to sit around in old blankets whilst their
wet clothes were dried. It was fun to nibble the ginger biscuits and
eat bread and milk. It was lovely to watch Comfort and Cheerful
putting down mattresses on the floor, and joking about who was
going to sleep at the edges and fall off.

"Are we very far from the Land of Far-Beyond?" asked Anna.
"It seems a very long way."

"Well – it isn't so far really," said Cheerful. "But because of
the difficulties on the way it always seems very distant. Cheer up –
you'll soon be there!"

The children slept well that night, and in the morning awoke as
merry as blackbirds in spring! They dressed in their dry clothes,
had breakfast of porridge and milk, and some fresh fruit from
Cheerful's garden, and then waited for Mr. Scornful. He soon
came along, quite merry and bright too.

"It's quite a tonic to spend the night with a fellow like
Courage," he told Comfort and Cheerful. "He puts heart into
me! I feel I can face anything now."

"Oh, Courage is wonderful in what he can do to people,"
said Comfort. "I've seen the most miserable wretches change in a
night once they met Courage. Now – are you ready? Here is food
for you. It will last out the day."

The six travellers said good-bye to their kind friends and once more set out on their journey. The sun shone again. It was warm. The Plain of Weariness was behind them. A pleasant country lay in front, full of brilliant flowers and singing birds.

They almost ran along. They were all quite determined that nothing, nothing whatever would make them turn away from the path that day. They would travel on and on – and maybe to-morrow they would come at last to the gates of the Land of Far-Beyond.

Soon they came to a little hill. "Can we go round it?" said Anna. "It's only a small hill but it looks pretty steep."

"The path goes over the hill," said Lily. "Bother! It always seems to take the most difficult way!"

"It can't possibly matter going round the hill instead of up," said John, who always preferred to take the easy way if he could.

"Well, it may matter, and probably *does*," said Mr. Scornful, and he took hold of John's arm. "We go *up* the hill my boy – so come along!"

And up the hill John had to go, though he sulked a little as he went. Half-way up they heard the sound of groans, and came across two people lying beside the path. Both of them were bruised, and one had sprained his ankle.

"What's the matter? And who are you?" asked Mr. Scornful, stopping beside them.

"We tried to cut up the hill just there," said the man, pointing to where it seemed as if a short cut could be made. "But the hillside gave way and we fell down here, cutting our heads, and bruising ourselves. I have sprained my ankle too, I think. My sister is hurt too."

"I am called Hasty, and my brother is Hurry," said the girl, who was weeping beside her brother. "We tried to get on our way as quickly as we could – and this is the result!"

"More haste, less speed," said Mr. Scornful.

"Oh, be quiet!" said Hurry, impatiently. "People are always saying that to us. We hate being slow. Only stupid people are slow. Look at that lot there, creeping up the hill!"

"Who are they?" said Peter, watching three people climbing the hill below them. They came very carefully indeed.

"The first one is Mr. Cautious," said Hurry, sitting up to look. "The second one is Priscilla Prudent – and the third is Mr. Careful. What a set of sillies they are! We started out with them, but soon left them behind."

"All the same, they will get to the top of the hill before you do," said Mr. Scornful. "Here you are, bruised and bleeding, unable to climb for a time at any rate – and they will certainly be at the top in an hour or two's time!"

"Help us up the hill," begged Hurry, standing up to see if his ankle would bear his weight. "Oh! My goodness, I *have* twisted my ankle! Give me your arm."

"You had better wait until your three friends come along," said Mr. Scornful. "I could give you a hand – but you would be too heavy, you and your sister, for these children to help. Wait for your friends."

"All right," groaned Hurry, sitting down again. "But oh, they drive me mad with their "Go more slowly! Don't rush at things! Take heed! Be prudent!" '

"There's a middle way in all things," said Mr. Scornful. "You needn't be too cautious, surely – but you need not be too hasty either! Well, we'll go on. Your friends will soon be here to help you."

The little party went on up the hill. They looked back after a while and saw that Mr. Cautious, Priscilla Prudent, and Mr. Careful had come up to Hasty and Hurry and were helping them up the hill.

"Well, that's all right," said Peter. "It will do Hasty and Hurry good to go more carefully for a bit! I'm glad we didn't have them as companions. It would have been most tiresome to have to race along with our heavy loads!"

They came to the top of the hill. They had hoped to see the Land of Far-Beyond from the top – but alas, it was hidden in blue mists that hung over the valley between. But to the right rose a very gay city!

"Look!" cried Lily, in excitement. "What's that place? Oh, do look at all the flags and banners! Doesn't it look gay? How I'd love to go there!"

"Maybe the path leads through the town," said John, longingly. "We'll see. Hark – I can hear bands playing too. Can you?"

Every one stood still and listened. Sure enough the sound of gay music played by bands came up the hillside and made every one's feet want to march and dance. It was a long time since the little company had heard music like that.

The flags and banners waved in the breeze. Shining towers rose up from the city, and glittered in the sun. "It almost looks like the City of Happiness, but smaller," said Lily. "Oh, I do hope we go there!"

"Come along down the hill and let's see if the path leads there," said Peter, eagerly, and the whole company went quickly down the winding path that led around the hillside, going lower and lower at each turn.

The path ran towards the gay town, and the children were delighted. They almost ran along it, so eager were they to get to the town and see the sights and hear the bands.

"What luck that the path goes to it!" cried Patience. "And what luck that there seems to be a feast or gala day on! This will do us all good!"

Just then there came the sound of rolling wheels, and horses' hoofs. The company turned and saw a most magnificent procession coming along their narrow path.

"Look at that marvellous coach!" cried Peter, in delight. "Is it made of gold? It shines as brightly as gold, anyway!"

In the carriage sat a broad man with a wide smile on his face. He was dressed very richly, and his mass of oiled curls fell heavily around his wide face. He waved to the children as his carriage rolled by.

Then came another carriage and then another. In each were wonderfully dressed people, all with amiable smiles on their faces, and all with waves of their hands for the staring travellers.

Men and women on horseback galloped by. They laughed and talked as they went, waving and smiling to the delighted children. Then the biggest carriage of all came rolling up – and to the children's great surprise and joy it stopped just by them!

In it were two handsome people, a man and a woman. The woman leaned from the carriage and spoke in a sweet but loud voice.

"Well, little ones! Are you, too, on your way to our beautiful city of Folly? How tired and care-worn you look! Would you like a lift?"

A servant standing behind the carriage hissed to the staring children.

"Have you no manners? Bow to her Highness, Lady Extravagance, and his Lordship, Sir Arrogance!"

The children bowed and curtsied. Lily spoke up at once.

"Yes, we are on the way to the city, Your Highness. Is it very far? We should very much like a lift if it is."

"It's far enough," said the lady, her great eyes brilliant as she looked down at the waiting company. "Arrogance, we can take these people with us, can't we?"

"As you like," said Arrogance, his handsome face looking rather annoyed as he stared at the travel-stained group below.

THE COMPANY SAW A MOST MAGNIFICENT PROCESSION COMING
ALONG

"But hurry now – we mustn't be late for the great Feast. After all, we are the guests of honour, you know!"

"I won't come in the carriage," said Mr. Scornful. "Let the children go."

"I think I'll not go either," said Peter, suddenly feeling that he didn't altogether trust this glittering company in carriages and on horseback. " I think I'll walk with Mr. Scornful."

"Well – I don't want to go without Peter," said Patience. "Anna, don't you go either. Keep with us."

The beautiful lady put out her hand with a kindly gesture and caught hold of Lily's arm. "Little girl, you are a pretty thing – come with me and I'll find you a dress that will show off your dark curls and your slim figure. Shall I dress you in red silk – or in blue satin? And you, little boy, with your merry face and dancing eyes – you shall have a cloak as grand as Sir Arrogance's with an edging of silver stars!"

Lily and John drew breaths of delight. "May we really have a lift in your grand carriage?" asked Lily, shyly.

The beautiful lady opened the door of her shining carriage and pulled Lily in beside her. "Come along," she said to John. "You shall join in the gala with us! You shall share the feast! Hear the bands playing to welcome us! What fun we shall have! Won't you really come too, you others? After all, you say you are going to the city – well, you can have a lift in the carriage behind, if you like!"

She shut the door, and her shining carriage rolled away with Lily and John beaming inside it. The two children were mad with joy. After all their hard travels it was wonderful to be in a great carriage and be whisked away to where music was playing a dancing tune.

Peter put his hands on his sisters' arms. "I know you'd like a lift too," he said. "But somehow I do feel we'd better not. After all, we know that the city can't be far away, because we can hear the bands playing. So it won't do us any harm to walk."

They watched the rest of the procession rolling by in grand carriages or galloping swiftly on great horses. Then when the last horseman had gone, the four set out together once again.

The music of the bands grew louder and louder as they came near to the great city. The flags flew merrily in the stiff breeze, and they could hear the laughter of crowds of people. A wall ran round the city, but the road ran up to a big gateway and disappeared under an enormous stone arch.

"We are nearly there!" said Peter, pleased. "In a few minutes

100

we shall be through the gateway – and then we'll go and find Lily and John, and have a great time with them!"

But suddenly Anna stopped in the greatest disappointment and dismay. Her face was so doleful, and her eyes suddenly so full of tears that the others were amazed.

"What's the matter, Anna? What is it?" asked Peter. "Quick! Tell us! Do you feel ill?"

"No," said Anna, tears falling down her cheeks. "No. But look – look!"

She pointed forwards and downwards to the path they were walking on. And the other three looked – and saw. The path did not go through the great gates of the merry city. It curved to the left – and went round the great city walls!

"It doesn't go through the city," sobbed Anna. "We can't go in! And oh! The music does sound so lovely!"

CHAPTER SIXTEEN

THE CITY OF FOLLY AND THE PEOPLE THERE. THE NARROW PATH. THE BACK-GATE OF THE CITY, AND THE SORRY FOLK WHO USE IT. HONESTY GOES TO FETCH LILY AND JOHN FROM THE CITY

Peter, Patience, and Mr. Scornful felt just as dismayed as Anna when they saw that the narrow path did not go up to the gateway. There was no real path to the gateway at all – only a smooth, slippery stretch of marble. The grassy path curved sharply away from this.

"Who would have thought of that!" groaned Mr. Scornful. "It really seemed as if we were being led right to the city – and it sounds such a gay place. I could do with some real fun – extravagant fun! I've thrown some money about in my time – and I suddenly felt I'd like to do it again!"

"Can't we go in just for a little while?" asked Anna, longingly. "We needn't stay. We could just go to the gateway and peep inside. I would like to see the band that is playing now. It makes me feel all jumpy inside."

"It can't matter if we just peep inside, can it?" asked Peter, turning to Mr. Scornful.

"I don't think we'd better," said Mr. Scornful, who was beginning to learn that it was easy to get into trouble and very hard to get out of it. "I really don't think we'd better."

"But what about Lily and John!" suddenly cried Peter. "They're in there! They went in that grand carriage."

"And they wouldn't notice that the narrow path curved round just here – because they wouldn't be able to see clearly where they were going!" said Patience. "They'll be in there waiting for us. What are we to do?"

This puzzled Mr. Scornful as much as the others. He suddenly made up his mind. "We'll just go to the gate and peep through it," he said. "We may see Lily and John inside. If we do we'll call them and make them come out."

So the four of them left the narrow path and went across the slippery, shiny stretch of marble to the enormous gateway. The gates were wide open. No gatekeeper stood there. Any one could pass in and out.

The three children and Mr. Scornful peered round the stone archway. A line of gaily dressed people were tripping past, keeping time to a band, which was playing loudly in a square nearby.

"It all looks and sounds such fun," sighed Anna. "Look at that lovely fountain playing! Doesn't every one look gay and happy!"

"Fireworks to-night! Fireworks to-night!" called a boy to Anna. "Come on in. Five thousand pounds of fireworks to-night!"

"And the fountain there is going to play wine, not water!" shouted another boy. "Come along in! There's money to burn here! Come and share it!"

A carriage rumbled through the gateway and the children made room for it, for it was very wide. In it sat a fat man, whose careless hands tore at the fine rug that covered him.

"That's Sir William Waste!" whispered some one to Mr. Scornful. "They say he built himself a house that cost a million pounds – and then had it all pulled down again because one of the taps in the sixtieth bathroom wouldn't turn on properly!"

"And there goes Lucy Lavish!" cried some one else. "Good luck to your Ladyship!"

The lovely lady in the silvery carriage took out her purse and threw money to the crowd around the gateway. They fought for the coins as they rolled here and there.

"And here comes Sir Squander!" yelled the crowd, as a fat horseman galloped up, his magnificent cloak flying out in the wind. "Salute to you, Sir Squander!"

Squander laughed a silly laugh and threw his wallet to the waiting crowd, who were on it like cats on a mouse. How they fought and scratched one another for the money in the fat pouch! Anna and the others looked on in disgust.

"I can't see Lily or John," said Anna, at last. "And, if we're not going in, we might as well go round the city walls, and see if there is some other way in that we can safely take. Then we may find the other two."

"You mean, the path might perhaps go in at another gate?" said Peter, eagerly. "I hadn't thought of that. You may be right, Anna."

So the four left the stone archway, and went back to the green, narrow path. They followed it as it curved round the city walls. They listened to the music and laughter that came from behind those great walls. How they longed to be there! Peter wondered if they had been foolish not to go. Everybody had gone in! No one but themselves had taken the other path.

Soon they came right round the city to the other end. Here there was yet another gateway, but not so wide as the first – and from it a sorry lot of people were stumbling and staggering!

Mr. Scornful and the children stood and watched in astonishment. Where were the grand and marvellous lords and ladies who had gone so gaily into that great city? Who were these wretched, diseased folk, people who limped and groaned, pale-faced creatures, sad, and sorry for themselves.

Three or four ugly-faced men ran about among the limping crowd, pretending to help them, but really feeling in their pockets to see if they had any coin or possession that was of any value. Mr. Scornful and the children watched them in horror.

Mr. Scornful caught hold of one man's arm and shook him. "Why do you pretend to help these poor wretches, and yet at the same time try to rob them of anything they have left?" he cried, sternly. "Who are these people coming from the back gate of the City of Folly – and who are you?"

"These people are the same kind whom you saw going in!" said the man, smiling in such a way that he showed his blackened teeth. "Ah, they go in gay and merry – but after a short or long stay in the city, they all come out like this! They don't know the wicked people there are in there, waiting for them. There is Disease and his many faithful servants. There are Robbery and Roguery, twin brothers who creep into the rich folk's houses and strip them of their goods."

"And don't forget that the demons of Boredom are at large

SQUANDER LAUGHED A SILLY LAUGH AND THREW HIS WALLET
TO THE WAITING CROWD

there too!" said another man, coming up. "And Malice and Spite go about with many others. Ah, the City of Folly looks a fine gay place, but its back gate is a sorry sight to see!"

Mr. Scornful let the man he was holding go free. He felt glad that he had not gone into the city.

"We are the servants of the Lord Disease," said the man, as he ran off. "We like to harry and vex all those who wish to escape from the City of Folly!"

"Oh, dear!" said Patience, looking at the pale-faced, thin, unhappy men and women coming from the gate of the city. "To think of poor Lily and John in there! How are we going to get them out?"

"Well, we certainly mustn't go in ourselves, there's no doubt about that," said Mr. Scornful, in his loud voice. "We've heard too much about the city to risk anything now. Perhaps we could send a messenger in at the gate to find Lily and John. If we could send a note to them maybe we could get them out before any-thing happens to them."

They looked around for a messenger. Coming down the path towards them was a tall, upright man, whose clear eyes were as blue as a spring sky. He paused when he saw the little party looking so worried.

"Are you from the City of Folly?" he asked.

"No, but we have friends there we want to get out," said Mr. Scornful. "But we don't know who to send in with a message. It seems to me that the city is a dangerous place for any one to visit. People go in merry and bright – but look how they come out!"

"It depends whom you send in," said the man. "Now you could send my friend Sensible in with safety. Nothing ever turns his head. And my other friend, Humble, goes in and out safely too. He hasn't any use for all that show and splendour. And you could send me in too. My name is Honesty. I'm not afraid of the rogues and scamps in there, and I always see through all the stupid waste and extravagance that goes on. I'll go, if you like."

"You're quite sure you will be safe?" asked Patience, anxiously, for she did not want this kind, blue-eyed man to fall into the hands of the dreadful people who seemed to live in the City of Folly, and ruin the stupid folk who went there.

"I shall be quite safe," said Honesty. "I am always safe anywhere. People always welcome me, even rogues and thieves!"

"Well – let me write a note to Lily and John then, and tell them to join us here," said Mr. Scornful, taking out a piece of paper from his wallet. "They took a lift in the carriage of Lady Extravagance and Sir Arrogance. Do you know whereabouts they were going to stay – because Lily and John would be with them."

"Yes, I know where they will be," said Honesty. "They have a house in the very heart of the city. "I'll take the note – and maybe bring the children back!"

Mr. Scornful scribbled the note.

"DEAR LILY AND JOHN,

"The path did not go through the gateway into the city. It is a terrible city, full of rogues, thieves, and evil things. Come away at once and go with the messenger, Honesty. Meet us outside the back-gate of the city at once.

"SAMUEL SCORNFUL."

He gave the note to Honesty, who saluted him and then made his way rapidly to the back-gate, meeting on his way another batch of sorry-looking folk, stumbling in panic from the city.

"I hope he won't be long," said Peter. "We have wasted precious time again. Lily and John will have had a narrow escape!"

The little party waited patiently by the back-gate of the city, filled with pity at the sight of the limping creatures who came out. And suddenly Peter gave a shout. "Here's Honesty! Look – here he comes!"

But what was this? Honesty was all alone. Where were Lily and John?

CHAPTER SEVENTEEN

THE TRAVELLERS GO ON THEIR WAY AGAIN. THE MADMAN CALLED INTOLERANCE. THE RIVER OF HATE OVERFLOWS THE BANKS OF PERSECUTION AND FLOODS THE TRAVELLERS. THEY ARE RESCUED BY CHARITABLE ON THE RAFT OF INDEPENDENCE

Peter ran to meet Honesty, who looked rather sad. "Where are Lily and John?" he cried. "Couldn't you find them?"

"Oh, yes, I found them quite easily," said Honesty. "They were in the house belonging to Lady Extravagance and Lord Arrogance. And what a fuss was being made of them, to be sure!"

"What were they doing?" asked Anna.

"Well, I got to the house, and went in," said Honesty. "All the doors in the City of Folly seem to be left open, you know! I heard the sound of children's voices, and went upstairs. There was a pretty little girl there, being dressed in blue satin. My goodness, her frock suited her perfectly – but she didn't look like a child in it, because it was made just like Lady Extravagance's own dress."

"Gracious!" said Anna. "What was John dressed in?"

"He was being fitted with a long, flowing cloak in red," said Honesty. "It had silver stars at the edge that glittered like the ones in the evening sky."

"John would like that," said Anna. "He always liked dressing up as a prince, when we lived in the City of Turmoil."

"Lily was eating a big plateful of cream cakes," said Honesty. "The cream was two inches thick! And John was trying to get through a whole ice-cream pudding by himself. He looked a bit yellow, I thought – as if he'd eaten too much already!"

"Did you give them our note?" asked Mr. Scornful. "Are they coming?"

"Yes – I gave them the note," said Honesty. "But they're not coming. They laughed at the note. They were rude and cheeky to me. The girl put out her tongue."

"How rude!" said Mr. Scornful. "She wants slapping."

"But – do you really mean they won't come and join us again?" said Patience, anxiously. "Why ever not?"

"Well, I suppose they think they are going to have a wonderful time now," said Honesty, "and so they will – for a time. But when their rich friends are tired of them, they'll be sent away and forgotten. Then, poor children, they will come wandering out of this gate, ill and sad."

"What are we to do about them?" said Peter, worried. "Do you suppose if *I* went into the city and found them I might be able to make them come with me?"

"No – nobody can make them leave the city except themselves," said Honesty. "They have already got the nasty ways and bad manners of those who live there. You must leave them and hope that they will find a friend if ever they come out again.

"Do you think you would look out for them, Honesty, whenever you pass by this gate?" asked Anna. "And ask your friends to look out for them too. Then you could perhaps give them a helping hand."

"I'll look out for them, certainly I will," said Honesty. "As a matter of fact, I befriend many of the poor wretches – some of them come to look for me, and I always help them then. Don't

THERE WAS A PRETTY LITTLE GIRL THERE, BEING DRESSED IN
BLUE SATIN

worry too much about Lily and John. I expect they will get tired of the city soon, and come out to look for you. Then I will set them safely on the road again."

"Thank you," said Mr. Scornful. "Well, we had better be going on. What a small company we are now – only four of us! And we were quite a crowd when we set out."

Peter, Anna, and Patience set out again rather sadly. It wasn't nice to leave the other children behind. But there seemed nothing else to do. The narrow path soon curved away from the city walls and went beside a gurgling stream. Soon they could hardly see the City of Folly, for mists came up and hid it.

They went on for a good way, and then met a man who called upon them to stop.

"You can't pass by here unless you tell me what is in your luggage!" he said, looking at the burdens on the backs of Mr. Scornful and the children. "Nobody takes luggage to the City of Happiness. So you must be carrying something you shouldn't."

"It isn't luggage," said Mr. Scornful, not at all liking the look of the man, who had rather wild eyes, and a hard mouth. "It's – well, I hardly know how to describe it – it's – just a burden we can't get rid of till we reach the Land of Far-Beyond. So pray let us pass."

"What's in the burdens?" asked the man, his eyes flashing. "You must tell me!"

"Oh, don't be silly," said Mr. Scornful, getting tired of the wild-eyed fellow. "Let us pass – or I'll knock you down. Who are you, any way?"

"I am called Intolerance," said the man. "I live here, not far from the path. I see travellers going by on their way to the City of Happiness. But a lot of them don't deserve to get there, and I try to stop them."

"What right have *you* to stop any one!" cried Peter. "You've no right at all! Let us pass."

"Tell me what's in your burdens first," said the man. Then, as nobody answered, he looked with his mad eyes at the loads on the travellers' shoulders. "Ah – I can see what is inside them! I can see!"

"You can't!" said Anna.

"I can see selfishness – and unkindness – and spite – and greed – oh, what terrible burdens! No one carrying those deserves to go to the City of Happiness!"

"I dare say we don't deserve to go – but we are going all the same!" said Mr. Scornful. "The Stranger told us that we might go there, and he should know because he came from there. You've no right to try to stop us."

"I detest the things you carry in your burdens," said Intolerance. "I hate sinners! I hate people who do not think exactly as I do."

"It is right to hate sin, but it's all wrong to hate the sinner," said Mr. Scornful, impatiently. "You're a sinner too because you hate people who don't think as you do! Now get away or I'll push you over!"

"If you dare to lay a finger on me I will open the gates of my dam over there, and flood the path!" shouted Intolerance, quite beside himself with rage. The others looked and saw that the gurgling stream beside which they had walked for a mile or two had now swollen into a rapid river that almost overflowed its banks. Near them was a stone dam which kept the river away from the path. In it was a sliding iron gate. Intolerance ran to open the gate of the dam.

"I'll flood you! I'll sweep you away!" he shouted. "You dare to threaten me – well, I'll show you what I can do. This is my River of Hate. I will let it overflow the Banks or Persecution, and sweep you off your feet. Then maybe you will crawl back to me and beg my pardon. You will say I am right, and will think as I do, and believe what I believe!"

"Stop!" yelled Mr. Scornful, as he saw the man turning a handle that lifted up the iron gate from the opening in the dam. "You're mad, fellow! Why try to drown people just because they are not what *you* think they should be! Stop!

But Intolerance was half-mad, and he opened the gate in his stone dam. With a rush the water poured out, sickly yellow in colour, and swirled around the feet of the four travellers at once. They yelled, and tried to run from it, going forward on the path as fast as they could. But the water followed them, licking round their knees now, pouring over the banks and down to the path.

"I hope it doesn't get any deeper," cried Anna, trying to keep her balance. "Mr. Scornful, yell to him to shut the dam."

But all the yelling in the world would not make Intolerance do anything he didn't want to! He stood beside the dam, shouting.

"I'll rescue you if you'll say you're sorry, and will agree with me!"

"Silly fellow," said Peter. The boy had found a firm place on the path, and had dug his feet hard into it to withstand the force of the water. "Anna! Patience! Come here to me and hold on to my arms. I'm steady here."

The two girls were almost bowled over now by the water, which had reached up to their waists. With Mr. Scornful's help they reached their brother, and held on to his arms.

"You're as steady as a rock, Peter," gasped Anna. "I was almost in the water just then! And goodness knows where it would have taken me! It is pouring away into the field over there. Oh, how horrid of Intolerance to treat us like this."

The water rose higher still. It reached to the children's shoulders, and up to Mr. Scornful's chest.

"We shall drown soon," said Anna. "Oh, Peter – don't you think we'd better yell to Intolerance to stop the river overflowing – we can easily say we're sorry, and that we agree with everything he says – even if we don't."

"Well, *I'm* not going to do that!" said Peter, holding his sisters very firmly indeed. "We've a right to think as we like, and to do what we think best. Why, Intolerance would be a real tyrant. if he had his way – trying to make every one think as *he* does! And see how wicked he is really, for all he pretends to hate evil things! He has nearly drowned us in his River of Hate!"

"The water's up to my chin!" groaned poor Patience. "I'm holding on to you, Peter – but the river is very strong."

"Look! There's a raft!" suddenly cried Mr. Scornful, and he nodded over the water, which was now a raging torrent. The children could just see the raft bobbing on the surface. On it was a sturdy youth, who was holding a rope in his hand, ready to throw it to any one caught in the flood.

"Hie!" yelled Mr. Scornful. "Hie! Can you save us!"

The youth heard his shout and threw the rope at once. Mr. Scornful gave it to the two girls, and the youth pulled them to safety on his raft. Peter swam to it and Mr. Scornful waded over and pulled himself up.

"Goodness!" said Peter, shivering "That was a most unpleasant adventure. Does Intolerance do this kind of thing often?"

"Whenever he can," said the youth, paddling the raft over the water. "But as soon as I see the water rushing over the path I get out my raft of Independence. It has saved many a traveller from Intolerance's River of Hate! My name is Charitable, and I'm quite the opposite of Intolerance!"

"I *am* glad you came when you did," said Anna, trying to squeeze the water from her clothes. "I should have been swept away the very next minute. I simply can't imagine how it was that Peter stood so steady!"

"Oh – your brother's name is Peter, is it?" said Charitable, his grey, wide-set eyes looking at the boy. "Well, you know what the name Peter means, don't you? It means a rock. So Peter is like his name, is he – steady as a rock when trouble comes along! That's good."

After some time the youth reached the end of the flooding water. His raft scraped on the ground and he jumped off. He helped the girls to the dry ground, and then waved his hand to where a big bonfire burned nearby.

"I always light that when I see the river flooding over the path," he said. "Then travellers can dry themselves."

The children and Mr. Scornful dried themselves gratefully by Charitable's big fire. It was a curious fire for it seemed to dry them completely in no time. Even their clothes underneath soon became dry. Charitable piled on more twigs when the fire died down.

"Why doesn't somebody punish Intolerance?" asked Peter, holding his steaming coat out to the flames. "He has no right to treat people like that."

"Oh, sooner or later he will be swept away in his own river," said Charitable. "And I don't mind telling you that I will not be out on my raft *that* day! He is the one person in the world I won't help, for he has persecuted others so often!"

When they were dry the four travellers sat down by the fire and shared some of their food with Charitable. He was a good companion, and liked listening to the tale of their adventures.

"Well, you're not far from the Land of Far-Beyond now," he said cheerfully. "You've got to go up the Steps of Impatience and past the Dragons of Fatigue – and then you're at the boundaries of the land you want. Good luck to you!"

CHAPTER EIGHTEEN

NIGHT-TIME. THE STEPS OF IMPATIENCE AND THE DRAGONS OF FATIGUE. HALF-HEARTED, AND PANIC AND TERROR. SLEEP AND REST COME TO FIND THE TIRED COMPANY

"I do like Charitable, don't you?" said Peter to the others as they set off down the path again, quite dry and cheerful. The flood-water had begun to go down, but they could not see Intolerance who was far away on the other side.

"Yes, Charitable is as good to be with as Intolerance was

hateful," said Anna. "It is a mercy that we find both good and bad along this road. If we found all bad I am sure I would have turned back."

"Well, we've no need to turn back now!" said Peter, cheerfully. "We're nearly there! Only the Steps of Impatience to climb, wasn't it? And some dragons or other."

"I don't much like the sound of the dragons," said Patience.

"Bless us all, you don't need to worry about old-fashioned things like dragons!" said Mr. Scornful, contemptuously. "Dragons! I didn't even know there were any nowadays. I must say I was very surprised to find that a giant was alive, too. I didn't really believe in him till I saw him."

"Yes – Giant Cruelty was a terrible creature," said Anna. "I hope I never meet *him* again! I'm glad that Mercy and Pity steal into his castle so often without his knowing it."

Talking cheerfully, they went along the way until the sun sank down. Mr. Scornful looked around. "I wonder where we could shelter for the night," he said. "I don't see anywhere. Perhaps we had better go on. We may see a cottage with a light in the window soon."

They went on and on. Suddenly the sun went and night began to fall. A few stars twinkled in the sky, but the night was so pitch-black that the children could hardly see their hands in front of their faces.

And then, in the dark, they came to the Steps of Impatience. It was just after Anna had lost her temper with Mr. Scornful.

Anna was feeling tired. She stumbled over a stone in the dark, and caught at Mr. Scornful's hand. He jerked her up rather roughly.

"Oh! You've nearly pulled my arm out!" cried Anna, crossly. "Oh, dear! Why didn't we find a nice place to rest in when it was light? Now we can't see a thing."

"Don't get cross about it. That won't help matters," said Mr. Scornful in a sneering voice.

"Don't talk to me like that!" cried Ann. "I'm tired. I want to rest. You shouldn't take us children on and on into the night."

"Oh, be quiet," said Mr. Scornful, impatiently. "I never did like children – always having to bother about them, and run round them!"

"Well, children don't much like *you*," said Peter, taking Anna's arm. "You're never kind or patient – you always sneer and jeer at others not so big or so clever as yourself."

They were all tired and cross. Each one felt irritable, and

113

wanted to quarrel – and just at that very moment they found themselves going up some curious steps!

They couldn't see what the steps were like in the dark – but they were very steep to climb up, and seemed to be clayey, so that their feet stuck to them.

"Oh, bother, bother, bother!" cried Anna, as she tried to go up quickly. "Why must these steps come just when it's dark and we are all tired?"

Patience remembered her name and tried to go up the never-ending steps patiently. But it was very difficult.

Peter lost his temper and stamped on one particularly steep step. "Horrid step! Of course you would be steep and sticky just as my legs are tired, and my burden is extra heavy! How I hate you!"

"I must say they are the most tiresome steps I've ever climbed," said Mr. Scornful, in a vexed tone. "It's so sickening not to be able to see them – or to see where we are going. We can't possibly stay and sleep on them. They are so steep that if once we fell asleep and rolled off one, we'd go bouncing to the bottom in no time."

Anna cried. Patience tried not to. Peter grumbled Mr. Scornful sneered at them all for grumbling, and for being babies. Every one felt unhappy and cross.

Suddenly, not far off, they heard a loud bellow. They all stood still in fright. Then there came the sound of another bellow and another. It was not like the noise made by any animal they knew.

"It's the Dragons!" cried Anna, in a panic. "It must be! Don't you remember that Charitable said we had to pass the Dragons of Fatigue? Oh, dear – to think we had to meet them now, when we don't at all feel like it."

The bellows came again. It sounded as if the dragons must be lying in wait a few steps above. What was to be done?

"They sound pretty fierce," said Mr. Scornful. "I don't know that I want to face them."

"We haven't anything to keep them off if they come at us, except our sticks," said Peter.

"I'm frightened and miserable," sobbed Anna. "Let's go back down the steps till to-morrow."

"What – and walk up them all over again!" cried Mr. Scornful in horror. "I should just think not. No – either we stay here on these steps till daylight comes – or we go up and face the dragons."

"Here comes somebody with a lantern," said Patience suddenly. "He's coming down the steps."

A voice hailed them. "Who are you? Why do you climb here in the night?"

"We are four travellers," said Mr. Scornful. "We have climbed up these tiresome steep steps – and now we hear the bellows of those dragons. We don't know if we can pass them safely or not."

"I shouldn't try," said the man, whose name was Half-Hearted. "I really shouldn't. Why, just now I warned two other travellers not to go by the dragons, and they did – and goodness knows what has happened to them!"

Suddenly the four travellers heard screams and yells coming from above. Then down the steps rolled and bounced two people, whose terrified shouts brought fear into the hearts of the children and Mr. Scornful.

"Oh, what's happened, what's happened?" cried Anna. Half-Hearted swung his lantern round and the children saw the staring eyes and wide-open mouths of a man and woman rolling by them down the Steps of Impatience. They were screaming loudly.

"It's Panic and his wife Terror," said Half-Hearted. "My word, how they scream! The dragons must have scared them terribly. Now don't you go on, will you?"

Mr. Scornful and the children really didn't know *what* to do. They couldn't stay on the steps. They didn't want to go down them to the bottom again. And they felt afraid of going up towards the dragons they could still hear bellowing.

"We'd better go up," said Peter at last. "Maybe the dragons are chained or something. If they weren't, surely they would be down the steps after Panic and Terror!"

So up the four of them went, very cautiously indeed, leaving Half-Hearted and his lantern behind. The roaring and bellowing of the dragons sounded very fierce as they drew near to them. At last they could see three pairs of eyes glowing like red embers in the pitch darkness.

"The eyes of the dragons!" whispered Anna. "Oh, I can't bear it! I don't want to go on. I don't care about going any farther!"

She sat down and wept. Patience began to cry too. "I don't think it's worth going on," she sobbed. "We never seem to get where we want to. It's always farther on."

Peter spied some one coming along in the darkness wearing a shining white robe that showed like the wings of a moth in the night. "Who is that?" he wondered. He called out, "Who's there?"

"It is I, Sleep," answered a calm voice. "I have come to seek you. My sister, Rest, is looking for you too. Charitable sent us word that you were coming."

At the sound of that calm, soothing voice, the two girls stopped crying. Sleep went up to them and put her soft arms around them. "Come with me," she said. "Rest is waiting for you, with warm, soft beds."

The four travellers followed Sleep upwards. She led them right by the bellowing dragons, whose red eyes gleamed wickedly in the night. "Don't take any notice of them," said Sleep. "They are afraid of me and Rest!"

The dragons stopped bellowing as Sleep passed by. The children sidled by as quickly as they could, dragging their tired feet along. They came to a little house in whose window was set a shining light that pierced through the darkness most invitingly.

Sleep's sister, Rest, pulled the children and Mr. Scornful inside. Not one of the travellers waited to undress or to have anything to eat and drink. They all fell straightway on to the soft white beds, and in a moment were sound asleep.

They slept all through the night, never once hearing the bellowing of the dragons outside, and quite forgetting Half-Hearted, Panic, and Terror. In the morning they awoke and stretched themselves lazily.

Peter jumped up and went to the window. He wanted to see the Dragons of Fatigue! But there were no great beasts to be seen, and no enormous bellows to be heard. How strange!

"Where are the dragons?" he asked Sleep, who came in to wake the others.

"Over there," said Sleep, pointing to a nearby glen on the hillside, where three small, strangely shaped beasts with snake-like tails lay asleep in the sunshine.

"What!" cried Peter in amazement. "Those *can't* be the dragons! They simply can't! Didn't you hear their enormous roars last night? Didn't you see their gleaming eyes?"

"Oh, you were tired last night, and couldn't see things properly," said Sleep. "The Dragons of Fatigue always look small and harmless in the morning, and there isn't a bellow in them. At night they frighten travellers with their roars, and make troubles seem bigger and harder. The best thing to do is to let Rest and me look after you for a night – and then things seem quite different in the morning!"

Peter looked down the hillside. He saw the Steps of Impatience stretching down and down. How steep they were! He turned to

SHE LED THEM RIGHT BY THE BELLOWING DRAGONS

look out of the other window, to the top of the hill. How far was it?

But they *were* at the top! At the very very top! And there, spread before them, looking not very far away, was the wonderful City of Happiness itself, shining brilliantly in the early morning sun! They were almost there! Yes, really, they were almost there!

CHAPTER NINETEEN

THE THREE PASSWORDS. THE GATEWAY OF THE LAND OF FAR-BEYOND. THE TWO GATE-KEEPERS. MR. SCORNFUL MAKES A GRAVE MISTAKE, AND IS LEFT OUTSIDE THE GATE. THE ANGELS OF THE CITY OF HAPPINESS. A TERRIBLE DISAPPOINTMENT

Peter called to the others in excitement. "Anna! Patience! Come quickly and see!"

The girls were soon at the window beside Peter, and gazed in joy at the shining city gleaming so brightly in the morning sunshine. Mr Scornful heard their excited chatter and came to join them.

Every one was cheerful and happy after a good night's rest. They laughed as they remembered Panic and Terror tumbling down the Steps of Impatience the night before.

"To think they were afraid of those silly little creatures over there!" said Peter, looking at the small dragons asleep in the sun.

"Well – we were rather scared ourselves," said Anna, honestly. "And I was so tired and cross and impatient that I really felt I couldn't put up with anything more!"

"It's no good going on if you're tired and cross," said Sleep, who had come to tell them breakfast was ready. "When people get like that they should come and stay in our cottage for a while, and get right!"

It was a happy breakfast-time. The four travellers joked and laughed, glad that the night was behind them, with those steep steps and the bellowing dragons. Now they could joyfully travel down the other side of the hill, keeping the shining city before their eyes.

"The boundaries of the Land of Far-Beyond are at the bottom of the hill," said Rest. "You will find great gates there with two gate-keepers. You will have to tell them the pass-words, or they will not let you through."

118

"But we don't know the pass-words!" cried Anna in a fright. "Oh, dear – how shall we know what to say? We simply *must* get through the gates."

"There are three pass-words to the Land of Far-Beyond, and its great City of Happiness," said Sleep. "They are pass-words given long ago by the Prince of the City Himself. The three words are – Faith, Hope – and Love. If you are asked which is the greatest of these, you must try to give the right answer – for each one must answer that for himself."

The four travellers said good-bye to their kind friends, and set off happily down the hill. It was an easy path, for the hillside was not very steep, and the path wound in and out through pleasant copses and thickets where birds sang loudly. The sun shone down and everything looked beautiful.

"We've had a hard time," said Peter, trying to shift his heavy burden a little, "but now it seems near an end. Oh, Anna – Patience – won't it be marvellous to enter the City of Happiness – and lose our burdens! We shall be able to dance and run again, we shall be light of body and gay of heart!"

At last they reached the bottom of the hill. Sure enough, just as Sleep and Rest had said, the boundaries of the Land of Far-Beyond were there. A wall ran to mark the boundary, and in it were great gates of beautifully wrought iron.

Towers stood at each side of the gate, and as the four travellers came near two men came from the towers. They had drawn swords in their hands, and a strange flame flickered up and down these weapons. The men had clear, piercing eyes, and they called loudly on the travellers to halt.

"Do you wish to pass through the gates?" asked the first gate-keeper.

"Yes, please," said Anna. "We are on our way to the City of Happiness because we want to get rid of our burdens."

"But no one is allowed in the city if they carry a burden!" said the second gate-keeper.

The little company stared at him in dismay. "But – but – we were told that we could lose our burdens there," stammered Peter.

"No one enters the city carrying a burden," repeated the gate-keeper, a flame gleaming on his sword, making it seem almost alive.

"Well – could we just go and see?" said Peter at last. "Could we pass through the gates and walk on to the city?"

"Only if you know the three pass-words," said the first gate-keeper, his clear eyes looking right through the boy.

"We do know them," said Peter. "They are – Faith, Hope, and Love."

"Quite right," said the man. "And now tell me, each of you – which is the greatest of those three?"

The children looked at one another. They remembered Kindly and Friendly, they thought of Comfort and Cheerful, they remembered Mercy and Pity – all of them had helped them through love and kindliness. Love must surely be the greatest of the three, since it could bring so much help and happiness to others.

"Well – I think Love is the greatest," said Peter, and his two sisters nodded their heads. But Mr. Scornful threw back his head and laughed.

"Love!" he said jeeringly. "As if Love is great! Love is silly and soft and no good at all. Good gracious me, if I'd loved my fellow men I'd never have got the riches and the power that I did get! Love doesn't get you anywhere."

"Do you need to get anywhere?" said the gate-keeper. "Ah, I suppose men like you must get somewhere! Well, tell me – which of the three do *you* think is the greatest?"

Mr. Scornful thought for a moment. "Well, I don't think much of Faith," he said. "But Hope isn't bad. I'm always hoping something good will turn up. I'm always hoping I'll make more money. Yes – Hope is the greatest of the three, *I* think!"

The two gate-keepers lowered their swords and beckoned to the three children. "You may pass through the gates," they said. "But this man may not."

The children passed through the iron gates as they swung open. But when Mr. Scornful tried to pass through, the gate-keepers stopped him with their flaming swords.

"You cannot pass," they said. "No man who scorns love and charity may pass on to the City of Happiness. You are a hard, unkindly man, and you still have many things to learn before you may go to the city."

Mr. Scornful tried to rush by the swords, but he was burnt by the flames, and with a scream he ran back. The gates closed slowly. The children were inside – but poor Mr. Scornful was outside.

Peter was upset. He had never been able to like Mr. Scornful, but it was sad to lose him just as they came so near to the city. The boy ran to the gate-keepers and caught hold of their arms.

"Let him through! He's come a long way, and gone through

120

TWO MEN CAME FROM THE TOWERS. THEY HAD DRAWN SWORDS
IN THEIR HANDS, AND A STRANGE FLAME FLICKERED UP AND
DOWN THESE WEAPONS

all the dangers and difficulties with us! It's his nature to be scornful and jeering. He can't help it!"

"We cannot break the laws," said the first gate-keeper gently.

"But can't you give him a chance?" asked Anna.

"He has had plenty of chances," said the second gate-keeper. "Every one has chances – a great many."

"But won't he ever get to the City of Happiness and lose his burden then?" asked Patience.

"There is another gateway to the Land of Far-Beyond," said the second gate-keeper. "It is far to the east, over difficult country. But maybe your friend will like to go to the other gate and try there. If he gets there, he will have learnt a few things he still does not know."

The children went to the gate and pressed their faces to the openings in the iron-work.

"Mr. Scornful!" shouted Peter. "Don't give up hope! There's another gate to the east. Go there and you may perhaps get in there."

"What's the good?" said Mr. Scornful, coming up to the gates, looking angry and disappointed. "I'm too old to learn new tricks! I'm going back to the City of Turmoil. I've got used to my burden. It doesn't feel so heavy as it did."

"But Mr. Scornful, it will get heavier and heavier if you go back to that dreadful place!" cried Anna. "Oh, do go on and try the other gate. We'll look out for you in the City of Happiness in a few days' time."

"Well," said Mr. Scornful, "I'll see. Maybe I'll try the other gate. Anyway – good luck to you all! And good-bye!"

The children watched Mr. Scornful walk away from the gates. He stood on the narrow path, as if wondering which way to go – backwards or forwards. Then, with a wave of his big hand, he turned up the path – to the east!

"He's going to try the other gate!" cried Anna, pleased. "Oh, good! I'm sure if he manages to get there he'll pass through all right. And we shall see him again some day. If only Lily and John were still with us! I wonder if they've left the City of Folly yet, and have met Honesty or his friends?"

"Well – only three of us left now," said Peter, looking down the path that led to the not-very-distant city. "I'm glad we managed to keep together and not lose one another. Come along girls. We're nearly there!"

It was lovely to see the gleaming city so near. It looked hardly more than two miles away. Surely there could be no more difficulties or dangers now?

"Doesn't it look lovely?" said Anna, looking at the shining towers that rose up to the blue sky. "And listen – I can hear bells!"

On the clear air came the sound of bells chiming together, making a tune. The children loved the welcoming sound.

"They almost seem as if they are ringing to welcome *us*," said Patience. "Oh, dear – I do so hope we shall be allowed in, after all. Do you suppose those gate-keepers were speaking the truth when they said that no one who carried a burden would be allowed into the City of Happiness?"

"We shall soon see," said Peter. "I can't imagine that any one would be cruel enough to keep us out, now that we are almost there! Surely it can't matter whether we carry a burden or not! Anyway, the Stranger did say that we would lose our burdens if we reached the City of Happiness."

"I suppose," said Patience slowly, "I suppose, Peter, that only happy people are allowed in – and no one is really happy if they have a burden like ours to carry. Perhaps that's it."

The three children drew nearer and nearer to the great city, and the ringing of the bells grew louder still. As they came near to the city, other people met them and joined them, all with happy, shining faces.

"Do you belong to the city?" asked Peter, shyly.

"Yes," said a kindly faced woman. "We have been away for a time, but now we are back, and how glad we are! The outside world is a hard place – there is so much that is unkind and pitiless in it – but how good it is to be back in the great city, where there is nothing but love and kindliness, pity and understanding."

"These children have great burdens on their backs!" cried a man in astonishment. "Look!"

Every one looked. The kindly faced woman looked sad. "You cannot go in if you carry burdens like that," she said. "You must take them off."

"We can't, said Peter. "The Stranger made them come – and he said they were part of us. But all the same, he sent us here – so surely we may go in?"

"You know the Stranger called Wanderer, do you?" asked a man. "He was sent to the City of Turmoil. Is that where you come from? Wanderer is back now – and he told us it was a dreadful place."

By this time the little company was at the entrance to the shining city, and the bells were very loud. There were no gates, only a great archway made of stone, set with precious metals that glittered wonderfully.

At the archway stood a company of strange beings. They had great white wings that curved over their heads, and their faces shone like moving water. They were almost too beautiful to look upon. The children blinked their eyes as they gazed.

"You cannot enter," said one of the angels, sorrowfully. "Your hearts are heavy with much wrong-doing. Your faces are sad. Only the good enter here, for only they are the happy."

The three children gazed at the angel with tears in their eyes. "Take our burdens away, and our hearts will no longer be heavy, our faces will no longer be sad," said Anna at last, in a trembling voice.

"We know we are not good," said Peter. "But no one taught us to be. Is that our fault?"

"I know nothing of that," said the angel in a troubled voice, and his shining face dimmed a little, so that the children could look at him without being dazzled. "I only know that you cannot enter here."

CHAPTER TWENTY

THREE UNHAPPY CHILDREN. THE WONDERFUL MAN. THE CHILDREN LOSE THEIR BURDENS AT LAST, AND ENTER THE CITY OF HAPPINESS. THE GREAT PRINCE OF PEACE AND LOVE

The three unhappy children turned sadly away from the archway, where the bright angels stood. What could they do now? There seemed nothing to be done at all. They walked away from the city entrance, and Anna cried bitterly.

Not far off was a stone bench. The children sat down wearily and looked at one another. "I suppose we must go back to our own city," said Peter. "But how unhappy we shall be there now. How we shall hate the cruelty and unkindness there, that once we thought nothing of! How we shall detest the selfishness and greed, the spite and the laziness!"

"And how we shall look for the things we now know are worth having," said Patience. "I shall remember Mercy and Pity – but we shall never see them in the City of Turmoil. I shall often think of Courage and wish he were with me."

"Do you suppose Mercy and Pity would let us live with them,

and help them each night when they go into Giant Cruelty's Castle?" said Anna suddenly. "I can't bear the thought of going back to the City of Turmoil and carrying this awful burden there for the rest of my life. Maybe it would grow lighter if we worked with Mercy and Pity, and did what we could for those poor prisoners."

"Well, we'll try," said Peter, cheering up. "Come on. It's no good staying here. It will only make us sad and unhappy to hear the sound of those bells that we thought were ringing out a welcome for us!"

He got up to go – but at the same moment a man came towards them. He had the kindest and wisest face that the children had ever seen, and they looked at it spell-bound. Who could he be?

The man spoke to them. "What are you doing here? Why do you not enter the city?"

"We can't," said Peter. "The angels with the shining faces won't let us. They say that only happy people may enter there – and we have burdens to carry, which make us unhappy."

"Do you so much want to enter the city?" asked the man.

"More than anything!" said Anna. "We have come so far, and have gone through so much danger to get here – and now we may not enter because we are unfortunate enough to carry these burdens. We are very sorrowful."

"Let me take your burdens and carry them for you," said the man.

"You can't do that," said Peter in surprise. "Don't you see – they are part of us! No one can carry them but ourselves."

"I will carry them for you," said the man, and he stretched out his arms to the astonished children. They went to him, and he pulled them down beside him on the stone bench.

Then the children did not quite know what happened – but in less than a minute all their burdens were taken from their backs – and the man had them on his! The three children stared in surprise and joy.

"My burden's gone!" cried Peter, and he leapt around as he had not done for a long time.

"Oh, I feel so light and happy!" sang Anna, and she danced as she used to do.

"It is wonderful to be free again!" cried Patience, her face glowing. She ran to and fro, feeling how marvellous it was to be free of the aching weight on her back.

The man sat watching them, his own shoulders bowed with the treble weight on them. But he did not look sad. On the

125

contrary, he looked happier than any one the children had ever seen. He smiled as he watched the children running and jumping. Anna ran up to him and took his hand.

"How did you take our burdens away?" she asked earnestly. "No one else could do it! And why did you do it for us? You have never even met us before!"

"Will you be able to enter the city yourself, now you have our burdens to carry?" asked Peter.

"You will meet me there," said the man, smiling. "Now go, children – and enter into the city at last. It is your city now, and you need never leave it again."

Happily the children ran towards the great archway once more. And this time the angels, seeing that the children had no burdens to carry, made way for the excited company and let them pass into the city.

How the bells rang out! How glad they seemed! How welcoming were the faces of all the people in the great city! There was nothing but gladness everywhere, and the children danced for joy. Their burdens were gone. They were free. They could live happily in this city, and need never go back to the City of Turmoil again; unless they, like Wanderer, went out to seek and help others. Maybe perhaps they could fetch their mother one day – and their friends?

But now they were too happy to think of anything but their joy at being light-footed and happy-hearted. The bells rang more and more loudly as the children made their way to the heart of the great city with its beautiful buildings topped by shining towers.

"Why do the bells ring?" asked Peter.

"It is to welcome the King's son," answered a happy-faced woman. "Look – come with me to the King's palace, and we will stand on the great steps to watch the Prince greet his father."

The children came to a wonderful palace that rose to the very clouds on high. Leading up to it was a marvellous flight of steps, and on these the woman and the children waited to welcome the King's beloved son.

The bells rang more loudly, and then the people began to cheer and shout. The Prince was coming, the Prince of Peace, the Prince of Love.

"Here he comes!" cried the watching people. And up the steps came a dazzling figure, whose face shone like the sun.

"What is his name?" whispered Peter.

"He is called Jesus," said the woman, astonished that the children did not know. "Do you not know Him?"

AND UP THE STEPS CAME A DAZZLING FIGURE

The children shook their heads – and then Peter gave a cry.

"But we *do* know Him! It was He who took away our burdens from us outside the city!"

The three children gazed in awe at the beautiful figure of the Prince of Peace. How could a Prince, the Son of the King, trouble Himself to take their burdens away and carry them Himself?

"He took away our burdens! See, He carries them on His shoulder now!" said Anna to the woman. She nodded.

"He carries the burdens of the whole world," she said. "Not only yours. He has enough pity and understanding, enough faith and love, to save the whole world."

The shining figure passed, and the children had to cover their faces, for they were dazzled. They were filled with awe and joy.

"To think we shall be able to live here for always!" said Anna at last. "How glad I am that we struggled on through all those dangers and difficulties to reach this wonderful city at last."

And there, among the ringing bells, we must leave Peter, Anna, and Patience, little pilgrims come home at last to the eternal city in the Land of Far-Beyond.